"Don't touch me."

Gabe quickly put up his hands in a motion of surrender. "I'm sorry." He wisely said nothing more, and Tessa tentatively moved closer again and finished cleaning the wound.

"That should do it," she said firmly as she picked up the trash and quickly cleaned the table.

"Thank you," he said softly in that disk jockey voice. "What happens next?"

"What happens is that we go over this case with a fine-tooth comb. We have to find out who paid that shooter, and how it's related to what was really happening at Southern Properties. If you really are innocent, you shouldn't have any trouble answering our questions."

He met her eye. "You can ask me anything you want, and I'll tell you the truth."

Her heart skipped a beat. *Why did you leave me at the altar without even one word of explanation? Did you ever love me? How could you deceive me like that?* She had lots of questions for Gabriel, but none that wouldn't reopen her own old wounds.

Kathleen Tailer is a senior attorney II who works for the Supreme Court of Florida in the office of the state courts administrator. She graduated from Florida State University College of Law after earning her BA from the University of New Mexico. She and her husband have eight children, five of whom they adopted from the state of Florida. She enjoys photography and playing drums on the worship team at Calvary Chapel in Thomasville, Georgia.

Books by Kathleen Tailer

Love Inspired Suspense

Under the Marshal's Protection
The Reluctant Witness
Perilous Refuge
Quest for Justice
Undercover Jeopardy
Perilous Pursuit
Deadly Cover-Up
Everglades Escape
Held for Ransom
Covert Takedown

COVERT TAKEDOWN

KATHLEEN TAILER

LOVE INSPIRED SUSPENSE
INSPIRATIONAL ROMANCE

LOVE INSPIRED® SUSPENSE

INSPIRATIONAL ROMANCE

Recycling programs
for this product may
not exist in your area.

ISBN-13: 978-1-335-72292-8

Covert Takedown

This edition published by arrangement with Harlequin Books S.A.

For questions and comments about the quality of this book, please contact us
at CustomerService@Harlequin.com.

Love Inspired
22 Adelaide St. West, 41st Floor
Toronto, Ontario M5H 4E3, Canada
www.LoveInspired.com

Printed in U.S.A.

For thou hast been a strength to the poor, a strength to
the needy in his distress, a refuge from the storm,
a shadow from the heat, when the blast of
the terrible ones is as a storm against the wall.
—*Isaiah* 25:4

To all of my wonderful readers. Thank you for taking time out of your busy day to spend some time with me! I hope you're reading this on a beach somewhere while watching a sunset or dolphins playing in the water. I am honored and grateful you chose my book to read.

May God bless you!

ONE

The first barrage of bullets hit the ceiling the second the shooter stepped out of the elevator. Dust and pieces of white fiber tile created a fog of smoke and littered the ground around the elevator doors. Screams ensued. Chaos reigned.

Gabriel Grayson heard the gunfire and quickly stood from his desk and hid by the wall, then took a quick look out the window that faced the main corridor of the real estate office. He watched, horrified at what he saw happening. Adrenaline made his anxiety almost palpable, and his heart felt like it was beating so rapidly it was going to come flying right out of his chest at any moment. Fear had been a constant companion three years ago when he had been a witness in a criminal case, and now the feeling was back and hit him in a rush, making it hard to breathe.

Ice seemed to flow through his veins, and he felt frozen, unable to even duck and hide, as the shocking scene played out in front of him. Two secretaries who had the misfortune of standing near the elevator when the shooter arrived went down during the gunman's second round of bullets, and Gabe's chest tightened as they fell to the floor, covered in blood. The killer aimed and fired a third round into the cubicles to his right, and papers, office supplies and bits of Christmas decorations flew up into the air as the semi-automatic rifle took the life of the accountant who worked at the desk.

A feeling of helplessness swept over Gabe as the shooter said nothing and stepped over the pieces of tinsel and red and green bows now strewn all over the floor. He was wearing dark clothing and boots, had a military bearing and a buzz cut of dark brown hair. Holding his weapon loosely he had a confidence and skill that were both intimidating and threatening at the same time. Moans and screaming ensued yet the man slowly brushed the ceiling debris off his sleeve and kept advancing, apparently unaffected by the death and destruction he was causing. He pushed the clip release button on his weapon as he walked and let the empty clip fall to the ground, then replaced it with a fresh one from his pocket as he advanced farther into the real estate office.

Gabe moved quickly away from the office window and opened his briefcase, then slid a stack of files inside. Every cell in his body screamed at him to flee, but doing something normal had a calming effect and helped him regain control of the anxiety surging through him. He'd already lost his past once before, and the files he was taking were vital to everything he had created in his new life. He closed the briefcase with a snap and glanced out his window to the rows of cubicles dominating this floor of the office building. The shooter had apparently turned to the right and was headed toward the computer server room. Gabe beat his hand impatiently against his leg as he considered the fastest and safest ways out of the building. His fists tightened involuntarily and he wiped away the beads of sweat that had popped out on his brow.

Another hail of gunfire sounded. He couldn't see it, but he could hear the uproar. Then he heard several loud noises, as if furniture was being moved violently from place to place. A large knot twisted in his stomach and his limbs felt heavy and frozen in place.

The shooting was getting closer.

Gabriel's heartbeat went even further into overdrive. He had to get out of here. Now.

More bullets sounded and spurred him into action, even as thoughts of Tessa McIntyre, and their previous life together, filled his memory. He had lost everything, even Tessa, his fiancée, when he had witnessed a politician's murder three years ago in Chicago and decided to testify against the assassins. He had sacrificed all he had to see justice done. Was history about to repeat itself? Was he about to lose everything a second time?

He sank to the floor, trying to hide against the wall so if the shooter passed the room and looked through his window, he would see an empty office. He hugged the briefcase to his chest and inched his way up, tilting his head at an awkward angle but trying to see out the window without giving his presence away. He had to determine if it was safe to try to make a break for it, and he felt his time was growing short. The office wasn't that large, and it wouldn't take the killer too much longer to reach his section. In his mind, there wasn't even time to call 911. Once he was out of the building, then he would make the call, if he was still alive to do it.

Why was someone shooting up their office? The horrific act didn't even make sense. Questions flew through his brain, and he considered and then discarded possibilities. They were a real estate company, not a bank or jeweler. They had nothing of value in the building. Why would anyone want to hurt them?

The screams suddenly seemed muffled, as if the shooter was moving in the opposite direction, and Gabe quickly got to his feet and glanced fleetingly around the door frame and into the hallway. There was still a cacophony of sounds coming from various parts of the office, but none in his immediate vicinity.

It was time to move.

He left his office and ducked behind a nearby cubicle wall and zigzagged around the water tank, then around the kitchen and the coffee station. He saw several people cowering under their desks or hiding under tables, but no one seemed to be paying any attention to him. Panic made it hard for him to breathe as he considered his options. He fisted his hands, then gritted his teeth as he motioned for a couple of other employees to join in his escape. Both shook their heads, their faces filled with terror. Gabe went a little farther toward the exit, his heart beating heavily against his chest as he worried about those he was leaving behind. He saw two female employees hiding behind the copy machine, and he sighed in relief when they came up behind him and joined his getaway. He said a silent prayer, asking God for protection, and the three of them ran the final few steps to reach the door at the back of the office.

The alarm sounded as he pushed through the exit, but he ignored the warning bells and ducked as he heard more gunfire. He didn't waste time looking behind him but tensed as a series of bullets hit the door above his head and left large, jagged holes in the metal, mere inches from where he had been standing only seconds before. Apparently, the gunman was not as far away as he'd hoped. One of the women made it out safely, but the second caught a bullet in the leg and fell into him, crying out in pain. He turned and grabbed her left shoulder, lifting and supporting her as he dragged her the rest of the way out the doorway, dropping his briefcase along the way.

Once in the stairwell, the first woman turned and grabbed his briefcase for him and then headed down the stairs, leaving him with both arms free to help the injured woman. She dragged her leg and tightened her grip on his arm, crying so hysterically she was barely able to help herself.

Still, he wasn't about to leave her behind. Even if helping her cost him everything, just like it had when he'd testified against those murderers in Chicago. He had to do whatever he could to save this woman, even though he barely knew her. Helping others without counting the cost had been ingrained in him since he was a child. He couldn't change those feelings, nor did he want to, especially since caring for others was an integral part of his faith.

The woman was still sobbing uncontrollably, and Gabe was at a loss as to what to say to help her focus on their escape. Words had never been his strong suit. Finally, he just swung her up into his arms and carried her the rest of the way down to the ground level. She burrowed into him, and he moved his head so he could see better to navigate the stairs.

"You can do this," he whispered fiercely, hoping his own determination to survive would bolster the woman's resolve. "We're almost there. Just a few more steps."

The woman ahead of them stopped when she reached the bottom and pushed through the exit door, holding it open for them. Noises and voices sounded from above them in the stairwell, but Gabriel ignored the din and followed the woman out the door. He didn't know if the shooter was right behind them or not, but he didn't want to wait around to find out. Once through the door, they found themselves in a deserted hallway on the first floor of the building. Gabriel set the injured woman down again and all three of them crouched against the wall, catching their breaths for a moment before moving on.

"The closest exit is down there," the uninjured woman said as she pointed to the left.

Gabriel nodded and took the woman's arm and pulled it over his shoulder, then moved so he could help support her as she hobbled. "Lead the way."

Seconds later, they pushed through the exit door into the parking lot.

"Freeze! Federal agents!"

Gabriel looked up and saw three men in FBI uniforms running toward them from a larger group of law enforcement personnel that had set up some sort of command post in the parking lot. A variety of police and FBI vehicles had swamped the area, and emergency lights bounced off the building windows. Gabe and the two women stopped, surprised. Gabe was amazed, not only that the police had shown up so quickly, but also that the FBI was involved and had already amassed such a large presence. His thoughts immediately went to Tessa and his eyes scanned the officers, looking for her blond hair and freckles, even though he realized she was probably back in Chicago, still working in their downtown office. A yearning he had never quite repressed swept over him as an image of her smile flitted through his brain. Even though three years had passed since he'd seen last seen her, he still missed her in his life.

Gabe pushed the thoughts of Tessa aside and made eye contact with the clean-cut man wearing an FBI jacket who was leading the pack. He let go of the woman he'd been helping and raised his hands. The man's gun was drawn, but at Gabe's motion he holstered his weapon and the three rushed up to help take them to safety. A few minutes later, the small group was securely ensconced behind a row of cars, and medics had started treating the injured woman. The lead FBI agent kept a protective stance in front of them, then turned once he seemed assured they were safely behind the cover of the vehicles.

"I'm Special Agent King. Tell us who you are and what's going on inside that building," the leader said, his voice filled with authority.

The two women looked over at Gabe, so he answered first. "I'm Gabriel Grayson. I was working at my desk on the third floor when a gunman came in and started shooting up the place about twenty minutes ago." He paused and took a breath. "The shooter looked military and was dressed all in black, but I only got a glimpse of him and didn't recognize him. I think his hair was brown." Gabe grimaced. "He reloaded at least twice. I don't know how many rounds he has with him. He's got some sort of semiautomatic rifle."

The woman who had been shot nodded, her face tearstained. "My name is Marcy Owens. I'm a real estate agent. I hid when I heard the shots and then followed Mr. Grayson out. I never saw the shooter. I was just trying to get out of there as fast as I could."

"I'm Katy Palermo. I'm an agent, too," the other woman added as she pushed some of her dark hair away from her face. "I followed Marcy."

"Is the shooter by himself, or is there more than one?" King asked.

"I think there's only one." Gabe shook his head, frustration filling him. "I tried to get a few others out, but they were too scared to follow me." The knot twisted tighter in Gabriel's stomach as he thought about the people he'd left behind. His assistant had stepped away from her desk, and he wasn't even sure if she was still alive or not. The thought of her losing her life filled him with trepidation.

"Did the gunman say anything to anyone?"

"Not that I noticed," Gabe said quietly. The others shook their heads in agreement.

"Did he seem focused on any particular person?"

"We couldn't really tell," Katy added. "His actions seemed kind of random, but I hid under my desk pretty much as soon as it started."

"What's in the briefcase?" one of the other agents suddenly asked Gabriel, pointing toward the satchel. Katy had handed it back to him as soon as Marcy had been helped and Gabriel had his hands free. Now it sat by his leg.

"Work. I don't even really need the stuff. It just gave me something to think about besides that madman in there who was shooting up the place. I don't even know why I brought it."

The agent raised an eyebrow but said nothing.

A moment passed. Then another.

"Open it," King directed. "We just need to verify you don't have a bomb in there or any other weapons."

Gabe wasn't thrilled with the man's tone, but he understood why the man had to ask. This was a deadly situation. Ensuring everyone's safety was a priority.

"Sure, whatever you need." He set the case on the ground and unlocked the latches, revealing the files from his desk, as well as a few pens and other office items.

The man checked all of the pockets, verifying there was nothing dangerous inside, then nodded at Gabe. "Okay. Close it up." He looked up and motioned to the west. "That ambulance is going to take you in for medical care," he told the injured woman. "You two will need to come with us until we can sort this whole thing out—" he met Gabe's eyes "—and you'll have to give me that case and the contents."

That surprised him. Why did the FBI care

about a bunch of paperwork? Gabe drew his lips into a thin line. "Why?"

"We're looking into some irregularities in your firm, and nothing can leave the building until our investigation is complete. We have a warrant that includes all of the company's files for the last three years. We were on the way to execute it when we heard about the active shooter." He paused and his forehead creased. "We also have some questions for you in particular."

"Questions? What kind of questions?" Even more trepidation ran through Gabe's veins. He knew he hadn't knowingly done anything illegal, but a mere three years ago, the two Montalvo brothers had assassinated a political candidate right in front of him in Chicago, and he had decided to testify against them to make sure they paid for their crime. He'd ended up in witness protection as a result. The thought of being involved in another investigation was not a pleasant thought, yet it seemed impossible to avoid. And how would this affect his new life? What were they investigating? As far as he knew, there was nothing unusual going on at the firm. They sold real estate. Period. Why was the FBI delving into their files? And why did crime seem to surface whenever he was around? Exasperation filled him.

He glanced back at the building behind him, and a muscle twitched involuntarily in his jaw. Did the fact that a shooter had just shot up his office mean that the Montalvo brothers had discovered his new identity and had come to finish what they had tried to do in Chicago—kill him for revenge? They had already made one attempt on his life, but had failed when the marshals who had been protecting him had drawn their guns faster than the Montalvos' hired mercenaries. The next thing Gabe knew, he had been whisked off to Atlanta with a new name and had been given a fresh start he had neither asked for nor wanted.

But if this shooter was working for the Montalvos, how had they discovered his new location, and why not just kill him alone? Why make the entire floor into a shooting gallery? It seemed unlikely that he was the target, but he needed more information before he could say for sure. Dozens of questions spun through his mind.

Gabriel met the agent's eye, trying to get any insight he could from the man's cryptic demeanor. "Do you know anything about the shooter or why he's up there?"

"Not yet."

That wasn't unexpected. Gabriel went in a different direction with his questions. "Well, what sort of pending investigation do you have with Southern Properties?"

"I'm not at liberty to say."

Gabriel considered the agent's answer, but once again decided to stay quiet. Right now, he doubted the law enforcement officer even knew about his background. Gabe needed to speak to the US marshal who had placed him in Atlanta before he trusted anyone else with his history. It was also clear that he needed help—help that might go well beyond what the marshal could give. He wasn't sure exactly what was going on here, but he was smart enough to know he couldn't face it on his own without assistance. Somehow, this day that had started off so normally had just turned into a living nightmare.

More thoughts swirled through his mind as anxiety pulsed through him. He needed to contact the one person who might be able to help him out of this mess. But what if she wasn't willing to come to his aid after what had happened between them? A new wave of emotion that had nothing to do with to-day's events swept over him. Would Tessa help? Someone had just tried to kill not only him, but every person on the third floor that worked at his company. This was big. And she was the one people called when mass shootings occurred. Her track record was unparalleled. He had to ask.

"I need to speak to Special Agent Tessa McIntyre. Immediately. She works for the FBI in Chicago."

Agent King snorted. "Yeah, right."

"I'm serious. Agent McIntyre is an expert in this type of case. She works in the homicide division."

"Maybe so, but this is Atlanta. We don't need outside help. We happen to have a very good homicide division of our own, as well as a financial crimes unit that has been investigating Southern Properties. You'll be speaking with them directly once we get you back to the office."

Financial crimes? Gabriel was so worried about the gunman who had injured and killed his coworkers that he was having trouble understanding why this agent was so focused on some sort of pending investigation. He turned his thoughts to the possibilities. What was going on at the office that was so serious it warranted the FBI's involvement? Nothing immediately came to mind, but regardless, he still needed help. He continued to push, putting as much conviction as possible into his voice. "Please contact Agent McIntyre anyway and let her know I asked for her. Okay? She'll want to speak to me. And I won't meet with anyone else but her."

King took the briefcase's handle with one hand and Gabe's upper arm with his other. "Let's go, sir."

Gabe gave a small jerk with his arm, trying to get the agent's attention. "Please, help me see Special Agent McIntyre. I know she'll want to talk to me. I guarantee it."

The man raised an eyebrow but said nothing further as Gabe accompanied him toward the waiting car. Fear continued to turn Gabe's stomach as he considered everything that had just happened. Was the shooter working for the Montalvos? Had all of those people that he worked with just been hurt or killed because of him and the case in Chicago? Or was this situation totally separate? Had he once again stumbled into a mess of someone else's making? Not knowing stressed him from head to toe, and he was also scared for his colleagues who remained inside the building. Guilt for the bloodshed started to raise its ugly head above all else.

Sonja Garcia, the Special Agent in Charge (SAC) of the Atlanta office, welcomed Tessa McIntyre and her partner, Chris Springfield, as she met them in the hallway outside the observation room that adjoined the interrogation room. She shook their hands.

"Thank you for coming on such short notice. You two made great time getting down here."

Tessa smiled, but hoped her stress didn't show. She'd been asked to help with tough cases before, but this was one for the books. Up until a few hours ago, she'd had no idea what actually happened to her fiancé when he had left her at the altar without a trace. Now he was involved in a horrific murder investigation that was only just beginning to unfold. Still, Tessa had to remain professional and detached. "We appreciate the special request for our help. As you know, our focus is on mass shooter cases, and we look forward to helping out your office and the US Marshals service in this joint endeavor."

Sonja smiled. "Were you adequately briefed?"

Chris nodded. "We received the preliminary paperwork and reviewed it on the plane."

Sonja led them into the observation room, and Tessa glanced through the one-way mirror at the man who was sitting alone in the interrogation room on the other side. He looked exactly like she remembered him. Short brown hair, athletic build, and wide, deep-set ocean-blue eyes. As she watched, he moved restlessly in his chair, obviously impatient. She glanced at her watch. The man calling himself Gabriel Grayson had been sitting there for almost four hours. No wonder he was antsy.

There, only a short distance away, was the man who had broken her heart a mere three years ago.

TWO

Sonja tilted her head and glanced at Tessa. "Has he changed much?" Her tone held a note of curiosity, and Tessa didn't blame her. All the local team had been told was that the director of the FBI had specifically requested that Tessa and her partner be brought in on the case to deal with Gabriel Grayson directly. On the surface, it looked like the FBI and the US Marshals had come together in the spirit of cooperation and multi-agency goodwill regarding the investigation of a protectee. Tessa had a prior relationship with the witness and had been brought in to assist due to that history and her expertise on mass shooters. That was the end of it.

But internally, there was a lot more to it, and Tessa was struggling. She pursed her lips but didn't answer immediately. Gabe looked up, and even though Tessa knew he couldn't see her through the one-way glass, she still felt a sliver of bitterness slide down her spine as she looked into his eyes.

Three years ago, Gabriel Grayson had been her fiancé, but he had left her humiliated and broken, standing at the altar. Not only had he failed to show up for the wedding, but she had also never heard a word from him since. There had been no explanation, no excuses, no recriminations. Nothing at all. Not even an apology. At first she'd thought he must have been the victim of a terrible accident, but after checking with all of the hospitals, and time passing without a word, she'd decided he must have simply changed his mind or fallen in love with another. Maybe he had never cared for her at all. Either way, he had decided he no longer wanted to marry her, pure and simple, and had left her disgraced and hurt beyond measure.

Her self-esteem had been shaky to start with, but the fiasco with this man had shattered it completely. She still felt unlovable, even now, three years later, and seeing him again twisted her stomach in knots and brought up all of those feelings of doubt and insecurity that she had thought she had finally put to rest.

Tessa had thrown herself into her work ever since that fateful day, and had reached professional heights that had helped her rebuild her life and her confidence. In fact, she was currently up for a promotion that was rarely offered to someone her age. Just looking at the man calling himself Gabriel Grayson, however, threatened to crumble the foundation of her success. As emotions swept over her like a roller coaster, her hands fisted and unfisted and her jaw tightened. She had had to take this assignment. If she had turned it down, it would have been professional suicide. As much as she wanted to pass on this case, she couldn't let this man ruin her professional life, too.

She had no choice.

She took a deep breath, then pushed her insecurities away and turned to the SAC. "He looks virtually the same." A muscle worked in her jaw as she turned to Chris. "Do you want the first crack at him?"

Chris shrugged, unaware of Tessa's internal conflict. He had been told the same information as the SAC—she and Grayson had a prior relationship, and that was the end of it. He didn't know the details, and Tessa had kept it that way on purpose, but she knew she'd eventually have to tell him. He was her partner. "I'll do it if you want me to, Tessa, but he specifically asked for you, so it might be better if you go first. We don't know much about Grayson's level of involvement with the white collar crimes. In fact, he might just be a victim of the shooting. Either way, you'll have a better chance of ferreting out the truth." He paused and flipped through the file. "Atlanta's Financial Crimes Unit says they think he's one of the money launderers at that firm, but they don't have any hard evidence against him. They've been investigating Southern Properties for a few months now and have been taking a hard look at Shawn Parker, the CEO. If Grayson is involved, you'll be able to get to the bottom of it, and you'll have this guy for lunch. You always do."

Tessa glanced back over at Gabe, who looked bored and had a frown on his face. Three years. It had been three years since she'd seen him last. Oh, how she had loved him! Seeing him again made the pain start bubbling anew.

But Tessa was a different person now. She was stronger. Wiser. And now most of that hurt had turned to anger. Determination to do her job and do it well filled her, even if the man on the other side of the glass had made it impossible for her to trust a man in her life ever again. She could do this. She would do this. And her feelings would stay bundled tightly inside her as she faced the man who had broken her heart.

Tessa pursed her lips and put her hands on her hips, pushing her emotions deep beneath the surface. Obviously, Gabe was neck-deep in this case, but despite their history, she had a hard time believing he was a criminal. No matter what his role though, she made up her mind to try to be as objective as possible. She was a professional and would do her job, regardless of the personal cost. As Chris had noted, they had been assigned this case. She and Chris were part of an elite team of homicide special agents, and they routinely got pulled into a variety of cases involving the most violent and serious crimes imaginable. They had been briefed by the Financial Crimes Unit on the plane and had gone immediately to the crime scene upon arrival.

She glanced back at her partner. She didn't look forward to explaining her history with Gabe to him. It was too embarrassing. The top brass knew about their past relationship, but they must have decided that the amount of time that had passed diminished the conflict of interest. Or maybe they were just testing her to see how she handled herself in a difficult situation. Anything was possible with the promotion on the line. The SAC position in Chicago that she was being considered for required a cool head and intense focus. Still, she'd have to tell Chris at some point. It wasn't fair to keep him in the dark. She opted for explaining everything later and looked back at Gabe one more time. "Okay. Fine. I'll do it." She squared her shoulders, gave Sonja a friendly smile and pushed out of the observation room and into the interrogation room.

Gabriel looked up at her as she entered, and astonishment swept over his features. "Tessa!" He stood and quickly approached her, but she put her hands up and took a step back, making it clear she wanted no physical contact with him. He moved back himself and dropped his hands by his sides. Confusion filled his eyes.

"Tessa, it's me. I'm so glad they found you. I asked for you but didn't know they could get you here so quickly. I know it's been a while, but…"

"Please sit down, Mr. Grayson." There was

steel in her voice that she did nothing to disguise.

He tilted his head, and his expression turned from surprise to bewilderment. He followed her directions and sat back down at the table, but his eyes never left her.

Tessa could tell he was studying her, but she avoided his gaze. The tension in the room felt thick and suffocating. She tossed the file folder she was carrying on the table and sat across from him, her body posture all business. His wide smile and perfect white teeth used to melt her insides. Now, just seeing him tied her stomach into knots. Painful ones. Once again, she tried to focus on the job at hand. "Mr. Grayson, you were brought in today because you were a victim in the shooting at the real estate office but also because you've been laundering money. We know you are a partner and real estate agent at Southern Properties, and we have uncovered at least three of your prior sales that are linked to accounts with straw companies that have been identified as fronts for illegal enterprises." Finally, she met his eye, and used an even tougher tone. "You're going to prison, Mr. Grayson. The only question is for how long."

He flinched at her words, and a moment

passed, then another. His dark blue eyes studied her and were filled with emotions she didn't want to identify. Finally, he spoke. "I think you're confused. I've never been involved with money laundering. Ever. I'm not a criminal. I was the victim at a shooting at my office this morning. I barely escaped with my life."

"I'm aware of that. That doesn't change the fact, however, that you would have been arrested this morning if the gunman hadn't intervened. If you help us out and are willing to testify, we might be able to work on getting you a lesser sentence for your crimes."

"Arrested? Crimes? That's crazy. You mentioned money laundering. I'm telling you I don't know anything about that or any other illegal enterprise." He leaned forward. "I sell real estate. My company sells real estate. That's it. We're not doing anything illegal." He shifted in his chair, obviously uncomfortable. "I've been here over four hours, and I'm tired and ready to go. Do I need to hire a lawyer?"

Tessa shrugged. "That's up to you." His voice was smooth as butter, just like always. She used to like that tone, but now it irritated her. He was thinner now than he had been three years ago, but his navy suit accented his tall, muscular build, and his dark hair was cut short in the military cut she liked so much. Even the paisley tie he was wearing brought out the sapphire color in his eyes—not that she'd noticed. She changed her focus to about a foot above his head so she wouldn't have to look at him directly.

"It's good to see you, Tessa," he said softly. "How'd you get here so fast? I thought you lived in Chicago."

Tessa gritted her teeth, trying to ignore the feelings his voice was evoking. She didn't want to be here. It was painful just to be in the same room with him, and it took all she had to stay rooted in the chair. She opened the file, ignoring his comment. "Let's start with the financial crimes, then we'll talk about the shooting. You were the agent in charge of the sale located at 256 Avery Lane that you closed on July 27…"

"Tessa…"

"My name is Special Agent McIntyre. Call me by my first name one more time, Mr. Grayson, and I'm out of here."

Gabe raised an eyebrow. His mouth opened and closed, as if he were actually shocked by her attitude. A moment passed, then another.

"I guess you're still angry, but what happened wasn't my fault. I can explain."

"Actually, I don't feel anything at all," she replied, although her tone belied her comment. Still, there was no way she was going to sit here and rehash the past—not now, and not ever. "Now, about that sale that closed on July 27—we have the buyer of record listed as…"

"I never meant to hurt you—" he started.

Tessa interrupted him by slamming the file closed and getting to her feet. "Save the lies for someone who cares," she said acerbically, meeting his eye. Two minutes. She hadn't lasted two minutes before she had wanted to strangle the man. Her anger management coach would not be pleased.

"I mean it. The last thing I wanted to do was hurt you." His voice took on an earnest tone and was for her ears alone. "I loved you."

"Oh really?" she replied, narrowing her eyes. She moved toward the door. "You had a funny way of showing it."

"I'm sorry, Tessa. I really am."

She put her hand on the doorknob.

"Please forgive me, Tessa. Please."

She paused and pulled at the black rubber band she had twisted around her wrist, snapping it against her skin over and over, but didn't look at him. The motion was supposed to help calm her down and stay focused, but it wasn't helping as much as she hoped. Emotions still swamped over her in waves, and her heart was beating frantically against her chest. Should she give him a chance to explain? She didn't want to. The scars he had caused were finally healed over. She did not want to rip off the scabs and sort through those feelings again. She snapped the band harder.

"What's with the rubber band?" Gabe asked softly. His tone was smooth again, like the voice of a disc jockey on an evening radio program.

"It's a coping mechanism," she replied succinctly. "I'm supposed to snap it anytime I feel like hurting someone in my immediate vicinity."

He ran his tongue over his teeth. His perfect, white, immaculate teeth. "I deserve that. I know I do. And much more. Just give me a chance to explain. That's all I ask."

Tessa scowled. Orders were orders, and she was an excellent FBI agent. Tessa was well-known as someone who would do whatever it took to get the job done. Her reputation was legendary and well deserved.

But now she was under a microscope, and everything she had worked for was in jeopardy.

Mustering her strength, she took a deep breath. She would force herself to talk to this man in front of her, despite the great personal cost. But she would do it on her terms, not his. Twisting, she turned and took her seat again. "I'm not interested in your explanations about the past, Mr. Grayson. Keep your comments to the relevant facts about this case. Any other topic, especially our history, is strictly off-limits. Got it?"

He studied her again for several moments but finally moved his hands in a small gesture of capitulation. "Whatever you say. It's your game now."

"You think this is a game?" She narrowed her eyes. and he wisely kept his mouth shut. She opened the file again and pretended to read the top sheet, even though she had the entire file nearly memorized since it had been handed to her earlier today. The Financial Crimes Unit had been investigating a group of companies that they suspected of laundering money for foreign criminals from Eastern

Europe and had discovered several irregularities at Gabriel Grayson's firm. They didn't know much yet about the gunman who had shot up the real estate office, except that he had died this afternoon when the FBI stormed the building. However, his fingerprints had shown up in one of the INTERPOL databases, and they had discovered that the gunman had European connections when they'd run his name through a cursory background check. His clothing was also European, and he had a pack of mints in his pocket that were a distinctly European brand. They were still in the early stages of the investigation of the mass shooting, but it was beginning to look as if the two cases were definitely linked. Criminals were notorious for using high-end real estate transactions to clean dirty money, but Tessa had never figured her former fiancé would be involved in something illegal or have these kinds of connections. Of course, she never thought he would leave her standing at the altar, either. Apparently, she didn't know him nearly as well as she thought she had. She tried to keep her thoughts objective though and fixed on the issues at hand.

"The gunman was killed today after he finished shooting up your real estate office, so we aren't able to interview him. We know he was Eastern European, but so far, that's about it. He killed six people and wounded several others."

Gabriel winced and looked genuinely moved by her statement. "I'm so sorry to hear that. Can you tell me which people died, and who was injured? I work with most everybody on the floor, and I've been really worried about them ever since I got out. We'll want to reach out to the families and do what we can to support them during this horrible time."

Tessa shook her head. "We can't say yet because we're still trying to notify the family of one of the victims." She leaned forward. "We also found a bomb in the main server room on the third floor. Thankfully, it malfunctioned and didn't go off when the timer stopped. We think the shooter was in the building to either set the bomb off himself or do what the bomb failed to do—kill as many employees as possible at Southern Properties and destroy your computer network." She put down her pen. "We think the gunman is related to the money laundering crime, which means he's also related to you. What we don't know is if he was targeting anyone in particular. Can you tell us why an Eastern European national would want to destroy your real estate firm?"

Gabe squared his shoulders and sat up straighter. He had obviously been surprised when she mentioned the bomb, but something in his demeanor had changed. "I have no idea. We sell real estate, mostly to wealthy individuals who purchase the properties as investments rather than for personal use." He paused and crossed his legs. "Apparently, there is a great deal of confusion going on here. I suggest you call the US Marshals office here in Atlanta and ask them about me. They should be able to answer all of your questions. Ask to speak to Joe Vahn."

Tessa's stomach tightened, just as it had a few hours ago when she'd first found out that the man before her had been in witness protection. It had been unexpected news, and she still hadn't had a chance to really process the information. "We've seen the summary."

A look of relief swept over Gabe's face. "Then you know my background. You keep asking me about the money laundering. I don't know anything about that. I truly don't. Nor do I know anything about a bomb, or a reason why someone would want to destroy the company." He drew his lips into a thin line. "You need to talk to Vahn. He can give you the details. Three years ago, I was involved with a case where a lot of people died. I have no idea if today's events are connected to that, or to something else, but it's something you might want to investigate. Hopefully, the marshal can shed some light on what's going on and we can get to the bottom of this."

Tessa raised an eyebrow. "Tell me more about the case three years ago."

"I'm not supposed to talk about it, but Vahn can. I suggest you call…"

"…the US Marshals office in Atlanta," she finished for him. She closed the file, stood and left him in the interrogation room without so much as a backward glance.

Gabe ran his hands through his hair in pure frustration. He was glad Tessa was here, despite her cold demeanor, but he missed the old Tessa he remembered. He thought about the quick smile and easy laugh she'd had when they had been dating. She'd had a serious side, but she'd also been playful and happy on a regular basis, and the joy inside of her had bubbled up and blessed him throughout their relationship. The last time he had seen her…

He stood and started pacing. She was nothing like that carefree, happy woman of the past. Now she was tough as nails and as unyielding as an iron bar. And on top of that, he felt like she had just poured a bucket of cold water on him. He knew he had hurt her badly. What he hadn't realized was how wounded she remained. And she was still suffering— despite her denials. It was painfully obvious in her body language and her furrowed brow every time she actually looked at him, which was rare, that her joy was gone.

Unfortunately, he hadn't been free to tell her the entire story when he had suddenly disappeared three years ago, and he wondered how much responsibility he bore for the changes he saw in her.

He had loved her. He hadn't meant to humiliate her, yet by all accounts, that's exactly what had happened. And to make matters worse, he had never been free to explain his actions, so silence had reigned between them ever since he had been swept into witness protection. In fact, this was the first time he had even seen her up close in over three years. WITSEC had rules that existed to keep the witnesses safe once they began their new lives, and the primary rule strictly forbid contact with anyone from their past.

His mind roamed through the details of the case that had forced him into witness protection to begin with. He had simply been in the wrong place at the wrong time and had observed the murder of a high-ranking politician by the Montalvo brothers—two hitmen he had testified against and were now serving life sentences in Illinois. If the mercenaries had discovered his new home, then he was as good as dead. They had not been pleased when he had testified, and he had no illusions about their power being diminished simply because they were in prison. If they wanted to kill him and knew his location, they would keep trying until they knew he was dead.

His thoughts moved back to Tessa. He could see the flame burning in her eyes, and he knew he was nowhere close to getting a chance to explain and apologize for the past. At this point, he was beginning to wonder if she was even willing to help him sort through this mess and the money laundering charges. And apparently, he needed her help desperately. Not to mention the fact that he was still in shock about the mass shooting that had taken place right in front of his eyes to people he knew and cared about. He continued to pace as thoughts, regrets and worries flowed through his mind.

About a half an hour later, Tessa returned to the interrogation room with another agent who she introduced as her partner. They both sat, so he took his seat again, too.

"So?" he asked.

"So, we talked at length to the marshal." Tessa started. "He gave us the full story of the Montalvos and about your assistance with that murder case."

Tessa looked upset, but her partner, Chris, kept talking before he could ask anything further about their conversation with Deputy Marshal Vahn.

"According to the marshal you are now our problem," Chris said in a matter-of-fact tone. "As of right now, you are officially in the protective custody of the FBI."

Gabe raised a brow. "What if I don't want to be in the custody of the FBI? I realize I need your help, but a few minutes ago, you were accusing me of a crime."

"And those charges are still pending, Mr. Grayson," Chris continued. "That hasn't changed. You can help the FBI with that case, or you can try to survive on your own and hope the Montalvo brothers can't figure out where you've gone. Either way, we're pushing forward with this investigation. This case is getting a lot of national press, however, and we believe that, if you help us, we can keep you safe and your true identity a secret. The choice is yours."

Gabe took a deep breath, trying to calm his nerves. "Am I under arrest?"

"Not yet," Chris replied.

Gabe pursed his lips. "I didn't do anything wrong."

"That remains to be seen," Tessa returned. Gabe glanced in her direction. She was still stiff and obviously uncomfortable. In fact, if he had to guess, he thought she was probably still chewing on the knowledge that he had been in witness protection. For now, he needed to back away and let her get used to the idea that he had reappeared in her life and was involved in her case. Then, if she let him, he would eventually explain what had happened back in Chicago and break down the details so she would understand why he had left so suddenly.

He had to make that right.

But he needed her forgiveness even more. He'd hoped enough time had passed that he could leave the past in the past and start fresh. Apparently, that was impossible, and thinking that way was probably a bit naive on his part in the first place. Time hadn't and couldn't fix the problems between them, but perhaps explanation and forgiveness could. He said a silent prayer that she would be open to the discussion and that God would help him know when the time was right to broach the subject.

A moment passed. Then another. He closed his eyes briefly, remembering the terrified faces of the people he had passed on his escape from the building just a few short hours ago. He added a prayer for the victims and their families. "Did that gunman today have any ties to the Montalvos?"

"We don't know yet," Chris answered. "The investigation is just beginning, but we're searching for any known associates and ties to other crimes. So far, we know the shooter was Eastern European and was a paid assassin for hire to the highest bidder. How that fits into the rest of case is unknown at this point, but we are investigating the Montalvo connection, as well as a few others that might exist. We hope to have some insight soon."

Suddenly, the door burst open and another

agent stuck his head in the room. He was a large man with a dark jacket and tie, and his face was both animated and filled with concern. When he spoke, his voice was grave and rumbling. "We just received a bomb threat. The boss ordered everybody to clear out of the building and convene down in the parking lot across the street. Now." He handed Tessa a manila envelope and stepped back out. Just as he finished speaking, an announcement went over the building intercom, confirming the news and ordering everyone to evacuate.

Tessa and Chris both stood immediately, and Tessa glanced inside the envelope, then closed it with the attached string. Although Gabe wasn't handcuffed, Tessa grabbed his arm protectively above the elbow as if he were a perpetrator and moved him toward the door. She hustled him out of the room and into the hallway with Chris following closely behind, carrying the folders they had just been reviewing in the interrogation room.

His mind danced. A bomb threat? What next? How had Gabe gotten on this crazy roller coaster again and lost total control of his life? He might not have been under arrest, but to him, protective custody seemed to be pretty much the same thing. He glanced over at

Tessa, whose expression was grim and uncompromising. How had things changed so drastically and gotten so bad in less than a day?

THREE

FBI staff directed the agents and other personnel like crossing guards as they hurriedly left the building. Some were carrying briefcases and other stacks of paperwork, and a few were escorting witnesses or others into the nearby parking lots. The staff had obviously been through evacuation drills and knew to check in with supervisors at predetermined locations so they could verify the building was empty. Tessa and Chris made sure their supervisor noted their presence as a bomb squad went against the flow and entered the headquarters, all dressed in protective clothing and carrying bomb detection equipment they would use to sweep the building.

Gabe occasionally glanced at Tessa's hand, which was still holding his arm just above the elbow. Did she think he was going to try to flee? Nothing could be further from his mind, but whatever the reason, he was glad to be near her and to have the contact, however minimal. There had been no one in his life since Tessa. Going into witness protection had helped put some very bad guys in prison, but it had also torn a giant hole in his heart. It had been the hardest decision of his life. He had stayed away because the rules required it, but now that he was near Tessa, it was as if he was alive again and all was right in the world, despite the antipathy she was showing and the horrific shooting at his office that had caused their lives to collide.

Someone jostled him from behind, and he glanced over his shoulder at the man who was already disappearing into the crowd. He was wearing a suit, like Tessa and Chris, as well as most of the men and women who had been in the FBI building, but Gabe checked his wallet, just in case. He couldn't imagine a pickpocket working in the parking lot after a bomb threat had been called into the law enforcement office, but this whole day had been strange. He breathed a sigh of relief when he remembered he didn't even have his wallet with him. The FBI had made him empty his pockets before they had put him into the interrogation room.

Another agent accidently bumped Chris's arm, and one of the files he was carrying hit the ground with a thud. Gabe bent over to help him retrieve the contents, just as a bullet flew by his left ear. If he hadn't bent at that exact moment to help with the files, he would have been killed instantly.

"Gun!" Tessa yelled, suddenly pushing Gabe down even closer to the ground and toward a nearby vehicle they could use for cover. Chris was seconds behind, and they both pulled their weapons and huddled protectively in front of Gabe as a volley of shots rang out. Another bullet hit the car behind them, and Gabe heard the ricochet, then felt something warm and sticky running down his forehead and into his left eye. He brushed at the liquid with his hand and came away with blood covering his fingers. Another bullet sounded, and a nearby agent cried out and grabbed his shoulder as he went down behind another car. More bullets cracked and hit the cars around Gabriel's hiding place. He was obviously the target of the rifleman.

"You've been hit," Tessa said softly, then pushed away his hand so she could get a better look at the wound. She holstered her weapon momentarily and held his head firmly in her hands as she examined the wound.

"It's not deep, but you might need a few stitches. I think it was just a ricochet."

"I barely feel it," Gabe said, surprised. He knew head wounds bled a ridiculous amount, but he was still surprised at his lack of pain compared to the amount of blood on his face and hands.

"That's the adrenaline talking," Chris said over his shoulder. "Let's get you out of here before the sniper gets lucky a second time."

There was yelling and controlled chaos in the parking lot as agents quickly responded to the gunman's threat. The shots seemed to have come from the upper floor of a nearby office building, and groups of agents had immediately converged and headed in that direction. Several other personnel had pulled their weapons and had found cover and defensive positions, but no one had identified the shooter yet, or his exact location, and no one was returning fire.

Tessa glanced in Gabe's direction before returning her eyes to the surrounding area, still searching for the sniper. "Looks like someone does want you dead after all," she said under her breath.

Gabriel had no response. He had never felt so helpless in his entire life, and it was not a feeling he enjoyed. He had almost been killed in his office, and now a marksman was shooting at him in a parking lot, all within a few short hours. Who could he blame? How could he fix it? Nothing came to mind, but something had to be done. He said another silent prayer, this time asking for safety for himself and all the law enforcement personnel in the parking lot.

A few moments later, Tessa grabbed his arm and motioned for him to follow her. They stayed crouched low to the ground but began weaving their way through the parked cars toward the rear of the building. They zigzagged around a dumpster and three black SUVs, and then Tessa led Gabriel to a blue sedan while Chris turned and kept his weapon pointed behind them, covering them from the rear as Tessa pulled out the keys. Gabriel was no expert, but he imagined the gunman had already disappeared by now and made his escape. Shooting into a pool of heavily armed law enforcement officers didn't seem like the brightest move, but it did show one thing—

whoever was trying to kill him was motivated enough to take outrageous risks. The gunman had just wounded at least one FBI agent and maybe even more. Now the Bureau would leave no stone unturned to find the killer because he had dared to injure one of their own.

Gabe jumped in the back seat, and the car was moving only seconds after he had closed the door. Tessa was at the wheel, with Chris joining her in the front as they made their escape. As they left the FBI headquarters building behind them, Chris immediately pulled out his cell phone and reported what had happened, then apparently received guidance for their next move.

"A safe house it is," Chris confirmed before hanging up the phone. He turned to Tessa. "Good thing you still have your go-bag ready and accessible."

"Are you kidding? Remember that last time when I had to go to court with only five minutes notice? I'm always ready. These days, I carry half of my wardrobe in that bag, just in case."

She smiled at Chris, and Gabriel fought a wave of jealousy that surprised him. He had no claim on Tessa, but it still hurt to think of her with anybody else, even if it was a platonic friendship with her partner. He wondered fleetingly if she was in a relationship with anyone. After all, it had been three years since they had been separated, and she was an attractive, vibrant woman. Despite their past, however, he didn't feel like he had the right to ask, especially after she had slammed the door shut on their discussion about their history in the interrogation room.

Chris smiled back and Gabe felt a measure of relief as he watched them more closely, picking up on cues and details. It became increasingly evident, by their tones and body language, that the two of them were friends and nothing more. He imagined law enforcement partners had to become close as they worked together. After all, they watched each other's back and spent long hours together doing a very difficult job. It would be only natural for them to become like a closely knit family, but Gabe couldn't help feeling relieved when he saw nothing romantic in their relationship.

Chris turned suddenly and handed Gabe a handful of napkins that he had pulled out of the glovebox, breaking his train of thought. "Sorry I don't have anything else to give you to stop the bleeding. We don't want to take a chance and drive you to the ER for that wound, but my boss assures me there's a first aid kit with butterfly bandages at the safe house."

"Works for me," Gabe agreed. The last thing he wanted to do was to give the shooter another opportunity to paint a target on his back. A safe house sounded perfect for the time being. He wasn't sure who was trying to kill him or why, but he didn't want to make it any easier for him.

It didn't take them long to reach the safe house, which was simply a small home in a nearby neighborhood in one of Atlanta's middle-class districts. The abode was simple, with few bells and whistles, but the area had several exit roads allowing easy access, as well as a quick escape if needed on the nearby interstate. Once they arrived, Chris immediately began doing a sweep of the surrounding area while Tessa grabbed the first aid kit and had Gabe sit at the kitchen table so she could examine his injury.

She took some cotton balls from a small plastic bag and dabbed them with hydrogen peroxide, then slowly started cleaning the wound. Her hands were shaking, and she just couldn't make them stop. She brushed some of his hair away so she could get a better look and also to give her some time to get herself under control. It was hard for her to be this close to him, and the air felt thick and made it difficult to breathe.

Oh, how she had loved him! Their time together had been some of the happiest of her entire life, yet when he had disappeared, her heart had been broken so severely that she didn't think she could ever love so completely again. Even now, her chest hurt every time she looked at him, and the pain and other emotions warred within her and tore her heart into pieces.

He reached up to lay a hand on her arm to steady her, but she pulled away quickly as if she'd been burned and took a step back, dropping the cotton balls as she did so.

"Don't touch me," she said more fiercely than she'd intended under her breath. She busied herself first with picking up the cotton and putting it on the table, then with moving the first aid supplies around as she got new cotton balls from the bag and once again dipped them in the peroxide. She flicked the black rubber band on her wrist a couple of times for good measure, then started dabbing the wound again.

Gabe quickly put up his hands in a motion of surrender. "I'm sorry." He wisely said nothing more, and she tentatively moved closer again and finished cleaning the wound. The gash was about an inch long but was close to the hairline, and she didn't think it would leave much of a scar. She could feel his warm breath upon her skin, and it sent a prickling sensation up her arm, but she did her best to ignore it as she applied the antibiotic and then the butterfly bandages to the wound.

"That should do it," she said firmly as she picked up the trash and quickly cleaned up the table.

"Thank you," he said softly in that disk jockey voice. "What happens next?"

"What happens is that we go over this case with a fine-tooth comb. We have to find out who paid that shooter and how it's related to what was really happening at Southern Properties. If you *are* innocent, you shouldn't have any trouble answering our questions."

He met her eye. "You can ask my anything you want, and I'll tell you the truth."

Her heart skipped a beat. *Why did you leave me at the altar without even one word of explanation? Did you ever love me? How could you deceive me like that?* She had lots of question for Gabriel, but none that wouldn't reopen her own old wounds. Knowing he had been in witness protection helped. But he had never mentioned any investigation or shared any concerns about criminals or upcoming trials that even hinted that he might go into WITSEC. Even if he had been trying to keep her safe, why hasn't he trusted her? How had she missed that? There hadn't been any warning at all that he would suddenly disappear from her life, especially on her wedding day. Had she really been that obtuse? She pulled roughly on the rubber band around her wrist as the thoughts spun in her mind.

Suddenly a door closed and Chris entered the kitchen and joined them. "The perimeter is secure." He pulled out a laptop and set it on the table, then adjusted the cameras through a simple computer program so they could see the outside of the structure from several different angles. "All the cameras are set and we're good to go."

Tessa pulled up a chair and sat down across from Gabriel, then opened a file on her phone as Chris sat at the head of the table and showed Gabe the picture. "Here's a photo of the man who shot up Southern Properties today. I want you to take a really good look at him."

Gabe complied, then handed the phone back. "I don't recognize him. I don't think I've ever seen him before today. He's not a client or anyone that I know through Southern Properties. Has the FBI learned anything new about him?"

"Details are slowly rolling in," Chris replied. "He's not affiliated with any particular group that we can find and seems to just be a gun for hire to the highest bidder. That also might explain why he wasn't able to make the bomb go off in your office. He might have oversold his ability to work with explosives. We're still working on who paid him for today's mass shooting, but we think you're right—we haven't been able to tie him to Southern Properties in any way so far."

"What about the Montalvos?"

Chris shrugged. "No connection there either, so far. But honestly, it's early yet."

Tessa set her phone aside and opened one of the files she had brought with them from the FBI office. "I still want to talk about the property that you sold on Avery Lane for 3.2 million dollars. It was quite the sale, and from what we can tell, it was bought with money from the Ukrainian mob." She flipped a page. "The same buyer bought two other properties, one on Peachtree Avenue for 4.3 million dollars, and another on Athens Road for 3.6 million. Our records show you've been working at that real estate company for at least the last three years, and during that time, you've become a partner in the organization. You're also their top salesman. Someone that high up in the hierarchy should have been aware of the nature of the companies you were dealing with. Questionable transactions like these shouldn't come as a surprise."

Gabe nodded. "Sure, I knew I was making some great sales, but I had no idea that some of the companies making the purchases were dubious, and I surely didn't know I was involved in laundering funds. BRT International was the buyer in all three of those sales, just as you say. I remember that because all three sales included money transfers from a new bank in Cyprus called First Financial that I hadn't used before. But the transactions each went smoothly, and I had no indication there was any problem with BRT. There are several companies with international ties that purchase real estate from us for investment purposes. Are you absolutely sure BRT isn't legitimate?"

"Yes, that's what we're telling you," Chris agreed, nodding.

"Tell us about Shawn Parker," Tessa requested, deftly changing the subject.

Gabe raised an eyebrow and his voice took on a protective tone. "Shawn is one of my business partners and actually is the one who introduced me to Andrew Bokova with BRT. He's the major rainmaker for our company."

Tessa pulled several photos from the folder and placed them in front of Gabe. They were all pictures of Shawn meeting with different men. "The FBI has been watching Mr. Parker for several months. During that time, he's met with several individuals with connections to the Ukrainian mob. Do you recognize any of these people?"

Gabe studied the pictures. "No, I don't know any of them."

Chris leaned back in his chair. "Shawn Parker has disappeared. Do you happen to know where he is?"

"As far as I know, he's been out of the country for the last two weeks on a business trip, and I haven't had a chance to speak to him in a while." He shrugged. "This morning, I tried once again to talk to Shawn because I had a question about a different sale, but it appears Shawn still isn't back yet. I left a message on his cell."

"Do you know where he went?"

"Western Europe. He said he had a consortium of buyers he was planning to meet with that might want to do some investing in the Atlanta area. He mentioned something about Spain."

"Try Donetsk, Ukraine," Tessa replied, showing him a manifest from a Turkish airline that boasted several flights to various Eastern European cities. "We have connected BRT with the Ukrainian mob, a group that specializes in prostitution and illegal arms sales. Their criminal activity generates dirty money that they've been using to buy high-end real estate through your company. Then they sell the property again a few months later, and the money is magically white as snow, while you and Shawn walk away with a fortune in commissions. Sweet setup."

"You and your partner have quite a bit of explaining to do," Chris added. "We have evidence that Parker's been working with BRT for over a year. And we know you are connected to those three sales we've mentioned, and maybe even more once we get a good look at your files. You were the listing agent, and the buyer's agent."

Gabriel sat back in his chair, his face white as the color drained away. If Tessa had to guess, she would have said his reaction was genuine. Maybe Gabe really hadn't known he had been working with mobsters or that one of his business partners was so heavily involved in criminal activity. He looked truly sick at the idea. She almost felt sorry for him. Almost.

"You have my briefcase, right?" he asked softly. "It contains the files from the recent sales I've been working on. Check out the buyers and the properties. BRT was only involved with one of the pending purchases, but that file should be in there with the others."

"We have it. It's in the process of being analyzed as we speak."

"Then you know what I'm saying is true," Gabe replied, his voice urgent this time. "Take a hard look at those files, and at all of my prior sales. I swear I had no idea there was a problem with BRT. There were no red flags."

Tessa fisted her hands, struggling as emotion swept over her. She'd thought she could stay focused on the case, but the more time she spent around Gabriel, the more she began to realize that she couldn't move forward until they rehashed the past. The pain was too front and center in her mind and consumed her thoughts, despite her best efforts. She wasn't going to be able to just ignore their shared history, as she'd hoped. She looked at Chris and raised an eyebrow, knowing it was time to be honest with him, as well. There was a question in his eyes as she took a deep breath and turned back to Gabe.

"The FBI obtained warrants this morning and has seized most of Southern Properties' computers. We have a team analyzing the data, and one way or another, we're going to get to the bottom of this." Tessa closed the file again and leaned back in her chair. "Here's what I do know, Mr. Grayson. You don't have a good track record of telling the truth. I know I can't trust a word you say— not now and not three years ago when you left me at the altar without bothering to give me an explanation."

FOUR

Chris raised an eyebrow at that comment and then suddenly stood and disappeared from the kitchen. He obviously wanted to give them some space to work out their personal differences, and Gabriel was thankful for the privacy. He'd been wanting to talk to Tessa about the past anyway, and she had just swung the door wide open. He watched Chris go, then turned back to Tessa and leaned forward. He wasn't going to waste the opportunity now that he finally had the chance to explain. He reached for her hand, but she quickly pulled away. He grimaced at her reaction, then pushed forward anyway. "I'm so sorry I hurt you, Tessa. I am. I know words can't really make a difference at this point, but I never meant to hurt you."

Her eyes narrowed even farther. "You're right. Those are just words."

Gabe leaned closer. "Then let me show you. I'm not a criminal. I swear I had no idea that Southern Properties was laundering money. I'll help you with this investigation in any way that I can." He paused and took a deep breath. "Allow me to make up for the past and show you just how sorry I am that I hurt you so badly. You know me, Tessa. I wouldn't have hurt you on purpose."

"I thought I knew you." She leaned back in her chair. "Then you disappeared." She drew little circles on the table with her finger, a habit he remembered so well from when they'd been dating. Her hands were always in motion. "So, here's what I think about this case before us. I think you and Southern Properties have been laundering money ever since you started working there three years ago. I think your partner, Shawn Parker, realized the FBI was closing in and ran off to avoid being arrested, and I think you were about to follow him when the shooter barged in and shot up the place today. That's why you dragged that briefcase full of files out of the building. I think the Ukrainians also realized the FBI was about to shut you down and decided to destroy Southern Properties and your computer network before BRT could be implicated and the connections traced and proven with documents from your servers. Then I think that once you were on the hot seat, you brought up your history with the Montalvo brothers so we'd start looking in the wrong direction and you could get off the hook."

She wasn't looking at him, but he noticed she was once again popping the black rubber band on her wrist. Her muscles were rigid and unyielding.

He shook his head, his jaw tightening. He was hurt and offended that she thought so poorly of him, but he schooled his expression and modulated his tone so he wouldn't express his frustration. "None of that is true. I'm in over my head here, but it's not because I intentionally broke the law. I'm shocked about Shawn. I can't believe what you're telling me about him. He and I are close. We've been friends ever since I moved to Atlanta." He paused and blew out a breath.

"Did the marshal tell you about the case I was involved in?"

Tessa shook her head. "Some, but most of the details were classified. All I know is that it involves the Montalvo brothers and the murder of Patrick Dwayne."

Gabe's brow furrowed. It was time to tell her everything, whether the WITSEC rules allowed it or not. "Patrick Dwayne was visiting Chicago the day of our wedding. He was running for senator."

Tessa raised an eyebrow. "And he was murdered in broad daylight down by Navy Pier during one of those pre-election meet-and-greets." She must have made the connection in her head because her eyes rounded. "You saw it happen?"

"I did. I stopped by the children's museum to pick up a last-minute gift for my nephew to thank him for being in the wedding and just happened to be in the wrong place at the wrong time. Ray and Carl Montalvo somehow got him away from his protection detail and had him cornered in one of those back hallways behind the vendors near the parking deck. I saw the shooting. They turned and fired at me, but I was able to escape unharmed. Chicago PD swooped in, I reported what I saw and the next thing I knew, my life had changed forever."

Tessa frowned. "And all the phones in the police department were broken that day."

Gabe shook his head at her sarcasm. "No, of course not. But they wouldn't let me call.

I asked repeatedly to use a phone, but they had me locked in an interrogation room the entire afternoon. Before I knew it, the feds were there, too. The Secret Service and even the US Marshals were involved right from the beginning. I wasn't even allowed to return to my apartment." He leaned back. "Nobody had ever seen either of the Montalvos before, even though they were wanted for over a dozen murders of prominent people all over the USA. They were infamous for their success at avoiding cameras and *never* left witnesses. I was an anomaly and would be dead now if the pistol Ray Montalvo pointed at me hadn't misfired. Anyway, for the next eight months, I lived in hotel rooms guarded by a rotating bunch of officers who made it clear I was not allowed to contact anyone from my past. When the trial was finally over and the Montalvos were convicted, they relocated me to Atlanta, and Deputy Marshal Vahn became my handler. I was still told that I wasn't allowed to contact anyone from my past. I checked out some sites anonymously on social media to get what information I could about you, but there wasn't much to find. Eventually, I figured so much time had passed that I was sure you had moved on anyway and wouldn't want to hear from me."

She shook her head and the frown hadn't disappeared. "Untrue."

Gabe reached across and covered Tessa's hand with his own, and to his surprise, this time she didn't pull away. "Please forgive me, Tessa. I know this was all my fault, and I made a big mess out of it. I should have found a way to contact you. I should have just taken somebody's phone and called the church or something." He sighed. "I had never seen a murder or even a dead body before. The whole thing was shocking and horrific. I'll never get those images out of my mind. But as bad as it was to see that, it was still worse knowing you were waiting for me at the church and I couldn't get there or even explain what happened. I knew it would hurt you, and that's the last thing in this world I would ever want to do."

She met his eyes, and for the first time today, she was looking at him with something besides anger and disappointment. He was encouraged and kept talking, knowing he might never get another chance to discuss this with her again. If he had learned anything, it was that his life could change in an instant and he needed to take every opportunity he could to tell the people around him his thoughts and feelings. "Please forgive me, Tessa," he said softly. "I've heard that unforgiveness is like when a person drinks poison and expects it to kill someone else instead. It eats you up inside, and the only person it truly hurts is you. After this case is over, you don't ever have to speak to me again if that's what you want. I deserve it. I know it. But I hope you can forgive me so you can move on with your life, and as long as you're simmering with hatred for me, you'll never be able to do that."

Tessa swallowed, and when she spoke, her voice was soft. "I don't hate you." She looked away from him, but when she turned back, he saw that she had definitely been affected by his recitation. The revulsion was gone from her eyes and had been replaced with emotions he couldn't quite define. He said a silent prayer of thanks to God for giving him this chance to explain what had happened so they could both move forward. He looked at her closely. Her shoulder-length blond hair was pulled back away from her face in a ponytail, making it easy to see her clear green eyes that were large and contemplative. He could tell she was mulling over everything he had just shared, and her next words even warmed him inside.

"I do forgive you, Gabriel. I see now that everything that happened that day was beyond your control. I wish things had been different, but I understand now that what happened wasn't your fault, and I was wrong to blame you. Thank you for explaining it to me."

He could tell by the softness of her tone that her words were sincere, and her forgiveness was real. The heaviness he hadn't even realized he was carrying suddenly fell from his shoulders. "Thank you for forgiving me, Tessa. I really am sorry. I wanted to marry you with all of my heart. We would have done well together."

She nodded. "Yes, we probably would have." She stood and drew one last circle on the table. "But now we'll never know." She turned away, and he sank back in his chair and watched her as she disappeared down the hallway.

Tessa was shaken by Gabe's words, and she paced in the hallway for a minute or two, then entered one of the bedrooms and shut the door behind her, trying to regroup. He seemed sincere with his apology, but if he really felt remorse for his actions, why hadn't he contacted her during the past three years?

Because he couldn't. She knew the rules the Marshals required. WITSEC was serious business, and the criminals he had testified against were deadly adversaries. He had done what was required to survive, and she couldn't fault him for it, no matter how badly his actions had hurt her. She felt as if three years of her life had been stolen from her, and yet no one was to blame besides the Montalvos, who were already serving time behind bars. She tugged at the black rubber band on her wrist, then pulled it off and shot it across the room and watched as it bounced harmlessly off the wall. The loss of her relationship with Gabe and three years of her life was a bitter pill to swallow.

She wanted to hit something, or at least do something physical so she could work off the stress and other emotions that were churning through her body.

Where did she go from here?

Gabe was back in her world, deeply involved in a very serious case, and she really didn't know how to deal with it appropriately. How could she be around him, protect him from his enemies and investigate his involvement in this case when she felt so many conflicting emotions every time they were in the same room together? She ran her hands over her hair and tightened her ponytail in a thoughtless motion, struggling with the sentiments she was feeling as the frustration filled her. Then she marched back and forth a few more times, mulling over his words again and again.

One thing had become clear: her anger had been clouding her judgment. Gabe had his faults, but manipulation wasn't one of them. He had also admitted that he'd been working at the real estate company without realizing that money laundering abounded. Gabe was an extremely talented businessman who was driven to succeed, but Tessa knew he'd never been one to cut corners. In fact, he'd always prided himself on the quality of his work. It must have been difficult for him to confess that he'd been pulled into something illegal with international implications, especially against his knowledge. She was starting to believe that he really was innocent in this money laundering scheme and was actually in a great deal of danger.

More restless energy pulsed through her,

and she continued her pacing. Despite all that had happened, regardless of the humiliation she'd endured, she also had to admit that she still felt attracted to the man. His dark hair and deep blue eyes made her heartbeat increase with a single look in her direction, and his voice was soothing and comforting.

But she had moved on. She'd thrown herself completely into her work, and had done so well she was now up for promotion as the new SAC of the Chicago FBI office. She didn't have time for a relationship. And even if she did, could she ever trust Gabriel Grayson ever again? That wasn't even his real name!

She fisted and unfisted her hands as the thoughts swirled through her mind. Her self-esteem had also been rock-bottom ever since Gabe had disappeared from her life. She hadn't had an easy childhood, and her mother had been more worried about the drugs she consumed than she had been about her own daughter's welfare. Her father had abandoned her at birth. She'd ended up in foster care and had always struggled with feelings of self-doubt and unworthiness. When Gabe had left her, she'd felt truly unloved and had decided she was never going to be good enough to have a personal life that wasn't filled with loneliness. She had finally accepted that.

She leaned against the wall that separated them and prayed silently for insight into this difficult situation. She needed God's guidance about how to move forward. Emptiness filled her, and she continued to pray. Finally, she pushed away from the wall and rejoined her partner in the living room, leaving Gabe alone in the kitchen.

Chris raised an eyebrow as she entered. "That guy was your fiancé?"

She nodded. "Yes."

"And he left you at the altar?"

She sighed. "Right again."

Chris shook his head. "Oh man, Tessa. I'm so sorry. I wish you'd said something sooner. I wouldn't have pushed you so hard to interview him."

She shrugged. "It's okay. I'm a big girl and I'll survive. It was three years ago, but I still should have told you. It's just something I don't like to talk about."

Chris turned and motioned toward the kitchen. "I don't doubt it." He paused for a moment, then asked another question. "Do you think he's telling the truth?"

"I do now," she admitted. "He just told me a lot more about the case. Several things I never understood finally make sense."

"How do you want to proceed?"

She shrugged. "*That* I'm still working on. Let's let him stew for now until we can find out what was in the files he brought us. I do know that a killer tried to silence him and everyone else at his real estate company, and then tried to kill him again in the parking lot. That has to mean somebody doesn't want him talking to us. He must know something, even if he doesn't know he knows it."

"What about the Montalvo brothers? Isn't that who he testified against when he went into witness protection?"

"Those are the ones, but so far, I don't see any connection. They were active in Chicago, but if they wanted him dead, why send a shooter into the real estate office? Why not just hit Gabe in the parking garage or at home when he's by himself? I didn't work on that case, but from what I've heard of them, they wouldn't have done something with so much collateral damage, and I also can't see them calling in a bomb threat and shooting at a guy in the FBI parking lot. It's something we should check, but it seems unlikely."

A moment passed, then another. Chris approached and nudged her playfully. "You going to be okay?"

Tessa grimaced. Chris was an excellent partner and was great at being supportive. Somehow, he usually knew just when to ask questions and also when to back off. His listening skills were one of the things that made him so good at his job. He was an attractive guy with blond hair and baby blue eyes, but Tessa had always thought of him as a lovable big brother. Their camaraderie and easygoing relationship was what made their partnership work so well. They had a genuine friendship and respect for each other's abilities. "I've been angry with him for so long that now I don't know what to feel, but I'll get through it somehow."

Chris nodded. "I understand. I wish we could pass this case off to another team so you could have some time to process all of this, but it just isn't possible. This case might help us get the answers we need to shut down that faction of the Ukrainian mafia we've been tracking up in Chicago."

Tessa straightened. "I'll do what I have to do."

"I know you will." He sat on the couch and pulled out his tablet. "You always do."

FIVE

"Garcia called and told me the bomb threat was a false alarm," Chris said in a contemplative tone that evening. "They swept the entire FBI building and didn't find anything." He pulled out his cell phone. "They've had access to the Southern Properties computers for several hours now. Want to call Jerome back in Chicago and see what he can tell us? Maybe he can give us a lead with his computer skills. You always say he's the best there is."

Tessa nodded and sank down into the chair across from her partner, thinking about the criminals they were hunting for the mass shooting and how they tied into the money laundering case they'd been investigating since they'd arrived in Atlanta. She and Chris had just gotten off a secure conference call with the Financial Crimes Unit, and they had discussed even more of the details as they were unfolding. The financial companies the FBI had been investigating appeared to be fronts for the Ukrainian mob, but the felons at the root of the case were proving to be incredibly elusive. Most of the money they'd been tracking had been coming through Cyprus, and that country had stiffer bank protections than even the Cayman Islands. It was almost impossible to get any records or banking information from the authorities there, so most of their trails died as soon as they hit the Cyprus connection. Despite several leads, they still didn't have enough evidence to pinpoint the mastermind of the operation, or even the sect of the mob that was involved, and they seemed miles away from making an arrest. Hopefully, something from the computers they'd seized from the real estate office yesterday would open the floodgates, or, at a minimum, point them in a new direction.

But stop them they would—of that she was certain, no matter how long it took. The Eastern Europeans they were investigating were master criminals who were disrupting commerce throughout the world, and she wouldn't rest until they were stopped and put behind bars. Their actions had hurt scores of innocent people, and it had to end.

Tessa waited while Chris made another secure connection with the video conferencing program and then propped his phone on the coffee table so they could both see the screen. A few seconds later they could see Jerome Renfrew, the young tech expert who seemed to live in the FBI's basement in Chicago. They had tied him into the work being done in Atlanta, and the case was now being handled as a joint operation between the two offices.

Jerome was working on one keyboard that operated a separate computer while talking to them on a different screen. Some people blurred their backgrounds when they used the Zoom meeting platform, but Jerome never did, and because of that, he usually came across as the absentminded professor. There were shelves of old computers and parts behind him, as well as other electronic equipment that were housed in the basement and formed his backdrop. The junky workspace, along with his distracted demeanor and inability to look anyone in the eye when he was talking to them, had earned him the humorous nickname Mole. To Tessa's mind, the entire room was a cluttered mess, but she couldn't fault the results. Jerome was a prodigy behind the keyboard, despite his unkempt appearance and thoroughly messy workspace.

"I'm not ready to talk to you two yet," Jerome reported as he took a swig of cola from his gas station refillable soda cup that had obviously seen better days. "I need more time."

"We've got a witness in protective custody with a target on his back and need to know something," Chris stated in a matter-of-fact tone. "We think someone tried to kill him twice today, and we'd like to know why."

"I've been working on Southern Properties' servers for a while now, but the files are encrypted. I'm close, though. Really close." Jerome hit a couple of new keys, then sat up straighter and leaned closer to his screen. "No!" he cried, his voice suddenly frantic. He began typing furiously, but his actions and body language revealed that he was unable to stop whatever catastrophe was obviously occurring right in front of him.

Tessa and Chris leaned closer to the screen, but neither one had any idea what was happening.

"What's going on?" she asked, her voice revealing the tension she was beginning to feel as Jerome started squirming in his chair.

"All of the data is disappearing, and I can't

stop it!" He pounded frantically on the keyboard, his fingers flying over the keys, but nothing that he did apparently stopped the screen from systematically erasing. A few seconds later, Jerome tilted the screen they were using for their conversation so they could see the screen he had been working on. It was empty except for a cursor that blinked ominously at them from the top left-hand section of the screen. Jerome leaned back in his chair, defeated. "I lost it all. We're back to square one."

"You mean everything off the servers is gone?"

"Yep. When I tried to solve the encryption on the files, I must have triggered a self-destruct sequence. I'm so sorry. It looks like it's some internal code. I bet the average users didn't even know it was there. They must really want to hide something from law enforcement to code malware like this into the programs."

Tessa turned to Chris. "What about the paper files Gabe mentioned?"

Chris shook his head. "I talked to Agent King while you were interviewing Grayson. He said his team has been studying them, but there wasn't much there."

Tessa closed her eyes and blew out a breath in frustration. Finally, she regrouped and opened them again. "We still might be able to find something he overlooked." Her words were hopeful, but Chris's look was skeptical, and she didn't really believe them herself. She knew the agents who had been analyzing the files. If they hadn't found anything, then there probably wasn't anything to find. A cold knot tightened in her stomach, and she could actually feel the tension growing within her. She was going to have to work with Gabriel. He was now their only lead.

A wave of stress tightened Gabriel's muscles and he fisted his hands. "Everything is gone off the servers?"

Chris nodded, while Tessa looked on from the corner of the kitchen. Gabe glanced over at her, and he could tell that she was carefully guarding her emotions. She seemed somewhat awkward and unsure around him now, which was unusual for her, and the news about the computer fiasco wasn't helping. He hoped they could work through this together and she wouldn't pull even further away from him as the case progressed.

"It turns out the files were embedded with

a security protocol," Chris continued. "They self-destructed when we attempted to get past the encryption. The FBI tech team was unable to stop it, and the Southern Properties drives were wiped completely clean. There's nothing left."

"I had no idea that encryption was on there. Our IT guy provided the computers for us already preprogrammed and ready to go," Gabriel said quietly.

"They probably didn't advertise it," Chris acknowledged. "A lot of companies actually do that sort of thing to all of their company computers, even their laptops, just in case one of their machines gets lost and ends up in the wrong hands. Corporate espionage is a whole separate course at Quantico. Anyway, the FBI will keep analyzing the paper files you provided, as well as anything else they were able to salvage from the raid on your offices. They probably won't find much though, since Southern Properties was storing everything digitally. They'll check the computers from your office too, but my guess is that those files will be encrypted as well, and will probably self-destruct just like the drives did. Meanwhile we'll focus on the shooter." He pulled out his phone and showed him a picture of the dead man's face. "Our research team just texted me some more about his background. His name was Adrien Metzger. Are you sure you don't recognize him?"

Gabe shook his head. "I'm sure. I've never seen him before."

Chris showed him a couple other pictures. "We've found some of his known associates. Do they look familiar?"

"No, no… Hey, wait! Go back."

Chris flipped back to one of the previous photos and Gabe nodded. "Yeah, I've seen him before. He's a friend of Shawn's. I don't know his name, but I've seen him hanging out with Shawn after hours. They go out drinking sometimes."

"Did you ever go with them?" Chris asked.

Gabe shook his head. "No, I gave up drinking when I became a Christian a couple of years ago. Bar-hopping just isn't my scene anymore, but Shawn goes out a lot on Friday nights. Sometimes Saturdays, too."

Tessa looked up, clearly surprised. "You became a Christian while you were in WIT-SEC?"

He nodded and gave her a smile. "I did. My faith has been sustaining me during the last few years. I really value my relationship with

Jesus. I've been going to a great church here in Atlanta over on Johnson Ferry Road, and I also joined a small group that does a weekly Bible study. It's been amazing."

"That's good news," Tessa acknowledged. She tilted her head slightly as she studied him, and he wondered what she was thinking. There were questions in her eyes, but she didn't voice them. Instead, she turned suddenly and pulled out the chair next to Chris. Then she took a seat and opened the file she had been carrying. "You said you thought Shawn Parker had gone to Europe. Do you know any more details about his trip?"

"Like what? You've already told me he went to Ukraine when I thought he was in Spain."

"When was he due to return?"

Gabe turned his full attention to Tessa, making sure his tone was soft and nonthreatening. He knew he had given her quite a bit to think about, and he wanted to try to put her at ease around him as much as possible while she processed everything he had told her.

"I thought he was due back last Friday, but it wasn't unusual for Shawn to extend a trip if things were going well. Like I said before, he is the primary rainmaker for the firm and has a lot of freedom to bring in the clients in any way he saw fit. If that required a few extra days of wining and dining, then he would stay and seal the deal."

She nodded, as if absorbing the information, then continued. "You probably already know a lot of this, but I'll start at the beginning." She pulled a photograph of a man with dark hair and heavy eyebrows out of the file and slid it toward Gabe. Shadows hid part of his face, but his features were still clearly discernable. "Do you recognize this man?"

Gabe shook his head. "No. Should I?"

"This is Alex Petrov, one of the key players in the Ukrainian mob," Tessa responded. "The FBI has been following his business transactions for about six months now. We know he's been dealing in arms and munitions—mostly in the Congo where they still have rebel factions ready to buy them. Once he gets paid, he's been making deposits in Cyprus and the Cayman Islands. One of the corporations we've been trying to tie him to is BRT International. He definitely has connections with key BRT personnel, and we think he's actually running BRT, but so far, we haven't been able to prove that, or any illegal activity. We think he's using that company as a front for his money laundering, but your company isn't the only one he's been involved with, and real estate sales isn't the only form of money laundering he's been using to clean his dirty cash."

She slid another photo over to Gabe, and he picked it up and studied it. There were two men in suits in the photo, and they were deep in conversation. One was his partner, Shawn Parker, and the other was Alex Petrov. A cold feeling swept over him as he looked at the photo. What was Shawn doing messed up with a Ukrainian mobster? He'd known Shawn ever since he moved to Atlanta three years ago and thought of the man as not only his business partner but also a good friend. Was all of this really possible? If so, how could he have misjudged him so egregiously? He hoped Shawn was just an innocent victim in all of this, but he was beginning to have his doubts.

Chris showed him a document from another file. "Your partner, Shawn Parker, is on the board of BRT. In fact, he drew up the articles of incorporation for that company and for three others that Petrov has been using to launder money." He showed him another document. "However, we're short on proof about the illegal transactions," he said in a flat tone. "It's not against the law to start a business. Every time we try to trace a payment though, we end up hitting a brick wall. We know Petrov is involved with Parker. We found other pictures where they vacationed together last summer in the Bahamas. We just can't prove the business connection in court, or the extent of Petrov's involvement." He opened a different file on his phone and showed Gabe a couple of snapshots that included Petrov and Parker in a tropical setting, enjoying the sun while boating and fishing. A few pictures included the same men eating dinner and conversing outside a hotel.

"Can you explain why your friend and business partner is meeting with a connected man in the Ukrainian mob?" Tessa asked briskly.

"No, I can't," he admitted with a frown. "When were these taken?"

"August of last year," Chris supplied.

"The FBI unit investigating your firm has plenty of evidence against Parker for several of the last real estate transactions. In fact, Shawn Parker was working for others beyond the Ukrainian mob, and they already have enough to get their convictions. If or when he's found, he will be arrested and charged.

What we're trying to do now is find out the extent of his criminal activity and how it relates to the Ukrainian mob and our shooter."

Gabe raised an eyebrow. "If or when?"

Chris hesitated a moment, then pushed forward. "I'm sorry to say we think Shawn Parker is dead. It's probable that the Ukrainians killed him to keep him quiet before we could tie him to Petrov and the Mafia. We're also thinking that is why the shooter destroyed your office yesterday and tried to blow up the computer records, just in case the computer encryption program didn't work."

Gabe sucked air in through his teeth as the news hit him hard. Shawn was dead, too? He leaned back in his chair as images from their friendship flashed through his mind. He remembered the day that Shawn had hired him, the day Shawn had given him a check for his first commission and the day Shawn had laughed with him and the other partners about their plans to expand the company during the next few years since business was booming.

Booming. It would be humorous if it wasn't so tragic. Apparently the only reason the company had been flourishing was because of Shawn's illegal activity. How could Shawn have gotten mixed up with such unsavory people? Nausea turned in his stomach as he realized the full implications of everything the two FBI agents were revealing. His new Atlanta life had been largely a lie, and he had gotten sucked in, hook, line, and sinker.

"I'm sorry," Tessa added. "I realize he's a friend of yours."

"A good friend. Apparently though, I didn't know him as well as I thought I did. Are you absolutely sure he's dead?"

Tessa shook her head. "No, we don't have proof. That's one reason we need your help. We think BRT is the key, and you've worked with them before. We need to find evidence that links Petrov and Parker and shows they did business together, not just vacations. So, I ask you again, do you recognize Petrov?"

Gabe fisted his hands. "I don't know Petrov, but I do know Parker, and I know a lot about our past sales. Yes, BRT sometimes accepted losses that other clients wouldn't, but I'm not as familiar with them overall as Shawn was. If everything you're saying is true, then the Ukrainians must have needed the money and the losses were acceptable and were probably offset by gains in other areas." He shook his head. "I'm just having a hard time believing Shawn was involved in anything illegal. Like I said, Shawn was the rainmaker for our company, and he brought me a lot of the sales that I was able to close. It's a big company, and there are at least two other partners who could be involved."

"We've looked into the other partners, but they only handled domestic sales, not international. They also didn't deal with BRT. That was Parker alone—and you, of course. And you must know something the mafia doesn't want you to share, or they wouldn't have tried to kill you yesterday in the FBI parking lot," Tessa said forcefully.

Gabe tilted his head. "Are you sure that was the mafia?"

Tessa shrugged. "We still haven't found the shooter, if that's what you're asking. He hightailed it out of there after he missed you. It was a wise move on his part. A parking lot full of FBI agents wanted his head after he took those shots this afternoon." She leaned back in her chair. "Why? Do you think it was the Montalvos instead?"

Gabe ran his hands through his hair. "I don't know. They have reason to want me dead, but the timing is strange. It seems more likely that the shooting at my office and the shooting at the parking lot are tied together."

"We agree," Chris said. "We're checking into the Montalvos, but I think the Ukrainians are the answer. That's where we should keep our focus."

Gabe grimaced. "Even with everything that happened with WITSEC, I've never actually been shot at twice in one day."

"I imagine you're going to be having several new experiences in the next few weeks," Chris said quietly, as he looked over at his partner.

Tessa nodded. "Being shot at might just be the least of your worries."

SIX

Could this situation get any worse? Gabe thought fleetingly. How had he finally gotten his life back together, only to become unwittingly wrapped up with the Ukrainian mob—an organization who apparently thought nothing of shooting up an office and threatening to bomb an FBI building? The idea was crazy. This day had been crazy. But as the nightmare unfolded, he realized there was nothing he could do to change the horrible series of events that had brought him back to a law enforcement safe house. He remembered that his pastor had once done a teaching on how people reacted when they lived through difficult times. They could either get bitter or better.

Gabe didn't want to become an angry, hostile man. He took a moment to pray and sort through the myriad thoughts and emotions flying through his mind. God would be with him, even though difficulties and situations tested his faith. This was a truth he knew deep within. The road might be rough, but God would never leave him or forsake him. He would never be alone. That thought gave him great comfort as he remembered the horrible events that had occurred today.

His mind returned to the shooting at the FBI building. If anyone could track down the perpetrators and discover who was responsible, it was the FBI. Shooting at their agents and calling in a bomb threat seemed like poking a sleeping bear. As far as he knew, the FBI had more resources than any other law enforcement agency in America. Someone, somewhere, in their rush to eliminate him, had just made a huge mistake, and it was one they would pay dearly for once they were caught.

And how could he have been so wrong about Shawn Parker? The man was an enigma who had apparently played him from start to finish. Even so, he hated to think that Shawn was dead, as well as all of the other victims of the shooting. So many had died. And for what? A pile of cash? It was hardly a reasonable quid pro quo. Life was precious, and much more important than money.

He glanced over at Tessa and watched her surreptitiously as she paged through the file. After arriving, they had spent the remainder of the day digging into the case, and her brow was furrowed as she concentrated and soaked up every word on the page. Regardless of the traumatic things that had happened recently, at least one good thing had occurred: he'd finally had a chance to explain his past behavior to Tessa McIntyre. He'd hoped they could have at least revived their friendship, but now, rather than anger, her attitude seemed to be one of detachment and indifference, as if they were merely passing acquaintances. His irrelevance in her life was a bitter pill to swallow, but what had he expected? Of course she had moved on. Her partner wouldn't reveal anything about her personal life, but he had let it slip that Tessa was due for a big promotion. He shouldn't be surprised that her life had changed. After all, it had been three years.

His eyes lingered on Tessa.

She was so beautiful! He loved the way her green eyes flashed as she talked and the way her straw-blond hair framed her face and accented her features, even when it was pulled back in a ponytail the way it was now. Her high cheekbones and porcelain skin only increased her allure, and the smattering of freckles across her nose gave her a playful appearance that added, rather than detracted, from her attributes. And when she smiled! Her face could light up an entire room. He hadn't seen her look at him like that since they'd been reunited, but he kept hoping a situation would arise that would bring out that amazing smile.

However, there was more to Tessa than her physical appeal. Tessa was also incredibly smart. It was one of the many attributes that had attracted him to her in the first place. And even here, in this stressful environment, she was cool and controlled, despite the emotional roller coaster he had caused in her life. Calm and professional—that was the image she exuded. He had always respected the way she handled herself and her difficult job. Because he had loved her so, the regret he felt now was amplified and felt like acid in his throat. She was such a wonderful person from the inside out. He hated the fact that he had hurt her so badly. How could he make it right?

He looked at her wrist and suddenly noticed that the black rubber band was missing.

Did that mean she had gotten over her anger and had truly forgiven him like she claimed? A wave of hope swamped over him. She had said the words, but true forgiveness didn't usually happen instantaneously, and it was obvious that the pain he had caused had run deep and long into every facet of her life.

Maybe, just maybe, God was also giving him a second chance to get his own life in order. And he needed it—especially now, when he was doubting his own ability to recognize when a person was leading him into trouble. Tessa was a straight arrow. He knew he had destroyed all hope of a relationship with her, but perhaps, if she was willing, she could help him through this mess and show him how to get his life back on the right track. He turned to her now and met her eye, filled with a new determination to rectify his past mistakes. "I didn't know I was laundering money, Tessa. I promise I'm telling the truth. All this time, I thought I worked at a legitimate business and that Shawn Parker was a trustworthy executive. I thought I was striving to make the company a success, not cleaning cash for criminals. Just tell me what I can do to make this right. I will do whatever I can to help you stop the offenders."

Her expression was still somewhat skeptical, so he followed his words with a quick prayer. *God, please help her open her heart. Show her she can trust me. Give me the strength to protect her and help her find the proof she needs to close this case.*

The prayer was short but heartfelt. He watched her carefully, wondering how she would respond, yet she said nothing for several minutes and simply studied him as if trying to gauge his veracity. "I'll take the first shift tonight," she said suddenly, breaking his train of thought. She stood and motioned to the clock. "It's late and we can pick this up tomorrow." She moved over to the surveillance setup and keyed into the laptop. It was as if she couldn't get away from him fast enough. Gabe gritted his teeth, then left Tessa with the computer and followed Chris, who was motioning him to come down the hallway with him. At the second bedroom door, Chris opened the manila envelope Tessa had gotten at the FBI headquarters and poured the contents into Gabe's hand. A set of keys, his wallet and some spare change came rolling out. The items had come out of his pockets when he'd first arrived at the FBI building, and he was glad to have them back. It gave him a sense of normalcy when everything else around him seemed like it was spinning out of control.

"Take the bedroom at the end of the hall. I'll be right here in this room. There are extra toiletries in the bathroom closet if you run out of anything. Stay away from the windows and make sure you keep the curtains closed at all times."

"Got it. Thanks."

Chris waved and disappeared into the bedroom, and Gabe went into his own assigned room and shut the door behind him. He hoped he could sleep but doubted he would get much. Too many images kept replaying over and over in his mind, as well as snippets from today's conversations.

Despite his doubts, Gabe was able to sleep for a few hours. He awoke the next morning, stretched and pulled himself up, feeling more refreshed than he expected to. He heard some soft noises coming from the kitchen, and after stopping in the bathroom, headed that way. Chris and Tessa were already up and were joking about Chris's cooking, and Chris was playacting with a spatula as if it were a microphone at a nightclub and he was giving a comedy routine. Gabe watched surreptitiously for a moment or two, enjoying their playful banter. He hoped someday Tessa would feel that relaxed around him again. He waited until Chris started singing a rock ballad from the '80s and then joined them from the hallway.

Tessa instantly sobered when he entered the room, but Chris pushed a plate of hot eggs, bacon and toast in his direction. "Well, maybe you'll appreciate my cooking. Tessa is apparently waiting for Bobby Flay to arrive and cook her breakfast."

"Now, hold on a minute," Tessa protested. "I just said I wanted the bacon cooked a bit more, that's it. Nobody likes soggy bacon for breakfast. Two or three more minutes, and it would have been cooked perfectly."

Gabe took one bite, then another, then winked at Chris and joined in on the teasing. "Hey, these eggs taste pretty good to me, and I'm loving the fact that I didn't have to cook it myself."

Tessa glared at him. "You're a lot of help," she said sarcastically, but there was a hint of frivolity in her eyes.

Chris took his own plate, a glass of orange juice and a jar of jelly and sat down at the kitchen table. "All right, princess. I leave the spatula and the pan to you. Help yourself and have fun cooking your own bacon."

None of them heard the first shot.

What they did hear was the coffee maker explode behind them. Chris quickly stood and then fell back as the second bullet caught him in the shoulder and forced him to the ground.

"Chris!" Tessa cried out and immediately pulled Gabe down beside her and under the table at the same time. Blood had sprayed from the wound and coated the wall behind him as Chris dropped to the floor. The third shot missed Tessa by a hair and drilled into the cabinet behind her, but she didn't hesitate as she grabbed Chris's body and pulled him back to safety under the kitchen table, as well. Adrenaline surged through her.

He groaned as she did so, but he must have understood what she was doing and tried to help her move his body weight, despite his injury. Once he was safe, she pulled out her weapon and fired twice in the direction the bullets had come from. She moved lower, then fired two more shots. Finally, she heard a shuffling of feet as the shooter retreated.

She quickly turned back to Chris. Her partner's face was racked with pain, and she squeezed his uninjured arm lightly as she examined the damage. The bullet had gone in the front and exited the back and had left a ragged hole in his black T-shirt. She hoped pieces of the fabric hadn't made their way into the wound, but all things considered, that small detail was the least of her worries.

"You'll live," she whispered, close to Chris' chest. "The bullet went clean through your shoulder."

Chris nodded then glanced around. "Did you see the perp?"

"No," she responded. "But he might still be in the living room. He backed off when I started firing at him."

"Go get him, Tess."

She nodded, understanding that despite his injury, Chris wanted her to go and stop the perpetrator before he hurt anybody else or escaped. She stood and used the walls for cover, heading toward the living room. She ducked and quickly put her head around the corner, searching for the gunman, her own weapon pointed at the ceiling. She caught sight of the gunman who was standing near the back sliding glass door and had disengaged the lock. She fired once and the door shattered.

"Freeze! FBI!"

Her words were drowned out by his return fire, and a series of bullets hit the Sheetrock where her head had been only moments before.

She tucked and rolled, then landed in a crouched position and fired three consecutive shots. All three hit the shooter center mass, and he grunted and dropped, right in the doorway. A strange silence ensued and she paused for a moment, just to make sure she didn't detect a second perpetrator. Hearing nothing, she finally rose and approached the prone assassin, her weapon still pointed at him, just in case. He didn't move. She used her foot to push his gun away from his outstretched hand, then bent to feel for a pulse. There was none. She studied his features for a moment but didn't recognize him. Finally, she holstered her gun and stood.

She pulled out her phone and reported what had happened as she quickly returned to her partner's side and leaned down beside him. "Are you doing okay?"

"So far," Chris muttered. Gabe had pulled a kitchen towel off the rack and was pressing it to her partner's shoulder just slightly above the vest, trying to stop the bleeding. The fabric was soaked with blood.

"The perp is down. I've called for backup and an ambulance, but I have to make sure he was acting alone."

"SOP," Chris said softly, using the acronym that stood for *standard operating procedure*. "Go. Gabe is a pretty good nurse."

Tessa grimaced at his attempt at humor. She was no doctor, but she believed the shot had probably damaged Chris's collarbone. It didn't seem life-threatening, but seeing her partner's blood everywhere was still her worst nightmare. And what if there were other shooters who had entered the house and were going to try to finish the job? What about Gabe? Fear and trepidation overwhelmed her, but she ruthlessly tamped the emotions down and focused on the job at hand. She would get through this, and if she had anything to say about it, they were all going to survive. She pulled Chris's gun from his holster and put it in his good hand. The heavy metal was cool and smooth and gave her a quick dose of reassurance. "Hang on and keep an eye out. I'll be back as soon as I can."

She left them and quickly but carefully checked the rest of the house and surrounding area. Thankfully, it appeared the gunman had been alone, but she had no idea if more were on the way or hidden somewhere in the neighborhood, just waiting for them to try to leave the house. She returned to Chris's side, and she was distressed even further to see how his skin had paled. He was losing way too much blood and was going into shock.

She grabbed a couple of blankets from one of the bedrooms and returned to cover him and elevate his feet. Chris' mouth worked as if he was trying to say something, and Tessa leaned closer, soothing him with his voice. "Don't you dare leave me, Chris. Just lie still and rest." She glanced over at Gabe, who was still crouched nearby. "Stay down. Help is coming for all of us." She kept one hand on Chris's arm, her other on the trigger of her Glock 9 mm, ready for action, just in case. Her eyes darted around the room as she considered what had just happened. How had the assailant found them? Her heart was beating against his chest as worry for Chris swamped her, and she fought the helplessness that she felt as her partner's blood seeped between her fingers.

She turned to Gabe. "Hand me another towel, please."

He complied and she replaced the blood-soaked material with the new one, pressing it carefully against Chris's shoulder.

She looked back over at Gabe as worry for his safety also filled her heart. Somebody out there didn't just want him silenced. They wanted him dead.

SEVEN

Tessa kept her weapon pulled and ready, just in case another perpetrator suddenly materialized. Unfortunately, from her position on the floor she wasn't able to see much, but now that she had done her initial sweep, she didn't want to leave Chris bleeding on the floor to check again. She listened intently for several seconds, but heard nothing except their own ragged breathing. For now, she would stay put and protect them the best she could with the remaining rounds she had with her.

"Get him out of here," Chris said between his teeth.

"I'm not leaving you," she fired back, glaring at her partner.

"I'm okay. Backup will be here soon, and there's nothing else you can do for me. Now go!"

She glanced over at Gabe, torn with indecision. Chris was right. Despite the seriousness of his wound, it probably wasn't life-threatening, and she needed to get Gabe to safety in case another shooter did materialize. The ambulance would also be here any minute. Her primary job was to keep Gabe safe. Still, it went against everything she knew to leave her partner bleeding on the floor.

"Go. Now," Chris urged. "Leave my gun with me, but take my extra clip, just in case you need it."

Tessa complied, removing Chris's extra clip from his belt and pocketing it. Then she and Gabe helped him gently sit up a fraction. They leaned Chris against the table leg so he would have a better view if trouble arrived before the help did. She moved his good hand that was holding the gun up to where the towel was pressed against the injury, so now he was holding both. "Keep holding pressure on that wound."

"I will. You have to keep Gabe safe," Chris urged. "There could be more of them on the way. I'm going to be okay. I promise." Chris nodded in encouragement, but his eyes were clouded with pain. "Make sure you...put on your vest."

Tessa smiled at him, hoping to divert his

attention from the throbbing pain the wound had to be causing. Chris had put on his bulletproof vest right before he'd started cooking breakfast, but the bullet had hit him right above it. Tessa's vest was still sitting on a chair by the kitchen table. "You got it. That's my next move. And don't think this little hole in your shoulder is going to get you out of making me lasagna some night like you promised. We had a deal." She spoke in a whisper, her eyes darting around as she spoke, all senses on high alert.

Chris rolled his eyes, his appreciation for her diversion attempts evident in his features. "I think getting shot is a pretty good reason to get me out of it. You…wouldn't like my food anyway. I'm really not that good of a cook."

"Anything I don't have to cook myself is fine with me. I'm ready to take a chance."

She glanced once again between the two men, then finally pulled out her phone and texted SAC Garcia to let her know the plan. Chris nodded, encouraging her. She listened once again, but still heard no signs of any other intruder. She inclined her head, motioning to Gabe to follow her, and headed toward the back of the house.

"Let's get you out of here," she said softly

to Gabe. "Follow me, but stay down." She crawled out of the kitchen, grabbing her vest along the way and quickly donning it before moving on. She could hear Gabe behind her, and they moved swiftly out the back door, closing it silently behind them. Once outside, the two of them bent low to the ground and moved as fast as possible, Tessa leading the way, with Gabe following closely behind. It was still early, but the sun was up and the sky was just filling with various shades of oranges and pinks. Tessa kept her eyes on their surroundings and her guard up as they moved. She didn't see any other perpetrators, but that didn't mean they were safe yet. They made it through the backyard of the neighboring house and then onto the street where there were a couple of parked cars.

She touched Gabe's arm to make sure he knew to follow, and Gabe nodded his assent. "Keep your eyes open," she ordered, her tone still soft but forceful. She saw nothing, but she heard boots against concrete in the distance. Were they friend or foe? She continued to use the cars as shields as they came up to a silver sedan. Tessa tried the door and found it unlocked, and she motioned for Gabe to get in once she had the door open. She continued to use her body as a shield to protect Gabe as he got in the car, keeping her weapon out and ready. "Move over to the passenger seat," she ordered. "Hurry."

Gabe nodded and slid across to the other seat, and she followed him in and quietly shut the door behind her.

"Do you think there are more of them out there?" Gabe asked.

"I have no idea, but we can't take a chance." She heard sirens in the distance, and she breathed a sigh of relief. Chris would soon get the help he needed.

She turned her attention to the car and checked under the mat, hoping the owner was old-school and left the key somewhere so she wouldn't have to hotwire it. She didn't find one on the floorboard, but a key and chain fell into her hand when she pulled down the visor.

"Thank God," she whispered softly.

"I already did," Gabe returned.

Tessa glanced over at him and gave him a small smile, then started the engine and pulled away. She drove for about ten minutes, constantly looking around her and using her mirrors to verify they weren't being followed. Her heart was beating rapidly against her chest as adrenaline pumped through her veins. She felt certain Chris would live, but driving away and leaving him hurt on the floor was one of the hardest things she had ever done.

When she felt they were far enough away to be safe, she slowed her speed and eventually pulled into a parking lot. Her hands were still shaking in the aftermath of the adrenaline surge she had experienced, and she rubbed them against her slacks several times as she slowly regained control. Finally, she got out of the car and called SAC Garcia, so they could have a real conversation that went beyond their texts. Gabe motioned as if he wanted to get out of the vehicle as well, but she waved the notion away and flattened her hand, hoping he would stay in the sedan and out of sight.

"Garcia," the firm female voice answered.

Tessa quickly updated her on the situation, describing the scene at the safe house and how she had borrowed the silver car, and, most important, asked about her partner.

"He's on the way to the hospital now. Preliminary reports look good, but he's going to be out of commission for a while."

"I can meet them at the hospital in twenty minutes."

"No, you can't," Garcia stated flatly, her voice like steel. "I need you to get Mr. Grayson to safety. His life is obviously in grave danger. Until we find out why and how all these pieces fit together, I need you with him to keep him safe."

"I understand," Tessa answered, "but…"

"No buts," Garcia responded. "Go to the safe house located at 342 Vine and await my instructions. The door code is 4317. We don't know how they found you at that other house yet, so for right now, your location is strictly on a need to know basis. That means you and I are the only ones with that information." She paused and her tone softened. "I know you want to be with your partner right now, but it's just not possible. Get Mr. Grayson to safe house bravo ASAP. We'll be in touch, and I'll send backup once I know it's safe to do so."

Tessa gritted her teeth. "Yes, ma'am." She glanced over at Gabe. "I'm heading that way now."

Gabe could see the concern for her partner written all over Tessa's face. He wasn't sure she would receive a comforting word from him though, so he said nothing, not wanting to make a bad situation worse. After all, this was his fault. He had been the target, and they both knew it. Her partner and the other agent hurt in the parking lot at the FBI building had all been collateral damage. He resolved to be as accommodating as possible so he wouldn't add any more stress to her plate. He was also thankful for each minute with her. It wasn't the time or place to try to rekindle their romantic relationship, but he hoped that at some point, they could at least work on their friendship and put the past behind them. A lot had changed in three years. He would settle for friendship, if it was offered. Right now, that seemed like a big enough hill to climb.

He looked up from his musings and was surprised to see that they had pulled into a department store parking lot. She shut off the engine and turned to face him.

"We're going shopping?"

"We are," she confirmed. "I admit the timing stinks. But I have no idea how they found us at the safe house, so from now on, we're done taking chances." She pulled out a small zippered wallet from her pocket and handed him a credit card. "Please buy a couple of new outfits and whatever else you need. You've got twenty minutes. I'll do the same. Then change in the bathroom and meet me back at the front of the store. Don't get anything flashy. The idea is to disappear."

He tried to hand back the credit card, but she refused. "I have my own wallet," he said, a touch of exasperation in his voice. "I can buy what I need."

"I understand," she replied, "but this card is untraceable. Keep it just in case you spend more than whatever cash you have with you. We can't take a chance that someone will find us by tracking your card."

He finally understood her reasoning and pocketed the card. "How do the clothes fit into the picture?" he asked, not sure about that aspect of her plan.

"I'm hoping I'm wrong, but I'm thinking one of us was tagged with a micro-transmitter. They're amazingly small these days and could be anywhere on our clothing. Change into whatever you buy, and then ditch what you're wearing now in the trash."

He nodded, grimly considering when or where he could have been tagged. The idea certainly seemed plausible, especially now in the technology age when all sorts of devices existed for purchase right off the internet. It probably wouldn't have taken much—just a quick touch to attach the device. Tracking someone for a nefarious reason had become all too easy. He watched Tessa head into the store. She walked with purpose. There was no other way to describe it. She was one determined person, and he loved that about her, yet he wondered if she ever took the time to relax. What did she do for fun during her downtime? Did she have a life outside work, especially now that she was moving up in the ranks? She had an incredibly stressful job that would affect anyone if they couldn't find a work-life balance. He remembered that she had always enjoyed decorating for the holidays, and he wondered if she still put out the Christmas lights and cross-stitched stockings like she had in the past. Tessa had always loved Christmas, and when they had been dating, one of her favorite things to do was to go out and admire the garlands and other creative displays that the stores and neighborhoods used to celebrate the holiday season. Today, the tasteful Christmas decorations around the store didn't seem to faze her, not even the snowflakes that fluttered from the ceiling or the big velvet bows on the walls. It was as if she was wearing blinders that kept her focused only on the path ahead. Maybe that wasn't too surprising considering her partner had just been shot, but it still made him worry about her. He hoped she found a release somewhere for the trauma she saw on a regular basis in her role at the FBI.

He shrugged and headed toward the men's department. He could ask himself those same questions. For the past three years, he had been on a wild ride of his own as he had tried to reestablish himself after the trial. It hadn't been easy. Yet his developing relationship with Jesus had been a firm foundation, and he had truly enjoyed his Bible studies as he had grown in his faith. He hoped he could talk to Tessa about it sometime before they went their separate ways. He paused for a moment and appreciated a beautiful nativity scene that was lit up near the main aisle, then continued on his way to find some new clothes.

He found what he wanted, went through the checkout line and headed to the bathroom. She was waiting for him by the front door of the store after he finished and he did a double take as he approached. Instead of the ponytail she usually wore, her sunny hair was down and fell generously around her shoulders, showing the soft red highlights that hadn't been as visible in the ponytail. Jeans and tennis shoes had replaced the telltale FBI suit, and she had donned a burgundy sweater that made her skin glow. Despite their circumstances, he couldn't help noticing that she had never looked lovelier. A warmth spread through him and gave him a strange sense of peace for the first time today.

"Ready?" she asked, already turning to leave.

He gave her the credit card and receipt, then held out another object. "Is this what you were looking for?" In his palm was a small black dot that looked like a speck of dirt about the size of a man's shirt collar button. The outside edge was rough rather than smooth and still had some adhesive on it that was left from when he had pulled it from his back.

Tessa's eyes lit up. "Yes. That's definitely a tracker. Is that the only one you found?"

"Yes, but there could have been more." He threw it on the ground and then smashed it with his shoe as he gritted his teeth. "I feel so stupid."

"Don't be ridiculous," she responded. "Anyone could have brushed up against you and put it on you. Even experienced agents wouldn't have felt it. My guess is they tagged you sometime while we were standing in that parking lot after the bomb threat got us out of the building. There were a lot of civilians out there in the mix. Now that we know that's one of their tactics, we'll take the necessary precautions."

"Yes, but your partner had to pay the price."

"He'll be okay, and we'll figure this out. That's a promise."

Gabe watched her turn and head toward the car with a growing sense of foreboding. He hoped it was a promise she was able to keep.

EIGHT

Gabe and Tessa made the trip across town in silence and arrived about half an hour later in a well-kept middle-class neighborhood with cookie-cutter small brick houses. She made her way to the back of the neighborhood that, oddly enough, had two other exits that he noticed, and then pulled into an empty driveway in front of a one-story home with a dark brown door. Leave it to the FBI to use a house that had several easy escape routes, he thought fleetingly. His real estate instincts kicked in, and for a moment, he actually thought about the selling points of the neighborhood. It was a banal thought, but he was glad that something was able to distract him, if even for a short time, from the fact that someone was trying to kill him.

Tessa parked and circled the car, reached in and helped him out of the back seat, then quickly ushered him into the house. Once the door was closed, she turned to face him.

"I need you to stay away from the windows and doors, got it?" she asked, her tone level.

"Of course," he responded, not quite sure where she was going with the conversation. Once again, she seemed to have put up a large barrier between them. "I'm really sorry about Chris. I'm glad your partner wasn't hurt any worse."

Tessa acknowledged his comment with a nod, but neatly changed the subject. "I need you to follow whatever orders I give you. My job is to keep you alive. I can't do that unless you cooperate."

"I plan to cooperate."

"I have to set up surveillance and check the perimeter," she said briskly, and she flipped on a few light switches and went farther into the house. "Don't touch any electronics without my permission besides the TV."

"Got it," he said as he followed her in. "I'm assuming there's food here, and I never had much breakfast. Can I make us some lunch?" It was almost noon, according to the clock on the wall in the living room, but even without his phone or watch to tell him, his stomach was letting him know that the two bites of breakfast he'd had were long gone.

She shrugged. "Knock yourself out. The FBI keeps these houses stocked, but it's mostly nonperishables. You'll probably find some meat and vegetables in the freezer and some canned goods in the pantry, but nothing gourmet."

"If I'm lucky, you'll at least have some basic spices."

She acknowledged his comment with a shake of her head. "Don't count on it."

She pointed him toward the kitchen, then turned, ostensibly to check and secure the house. He made his way to the kitchen and opened the fridge and freezer, checking to see what he had to work with. He was no expert, but he found some vacuum-packed frozen chicken and broccoli and pulled them out, as well as a package of alfredo noodles, a can of evaporated milk and a container of parmesan cheese. He searched for and found some garlic cloves that were still fresh and a black pepper grinder and went to work.

About ten minutes into his cooking, Tessa returned with a laptop that had a sticker on the top that said it belonged to the house. She set it on the counter that separated the kitchen from the living room, then went to the desktop that was set up in the corner of the kitchen and powered it on. An intricate surveillance system popped up on the screen, and he could see that cameras has been strategically placed around the building so they would have a good view of anyone approaching the house. She continued working on the desktop and basically ignored him while he concentrated on fixing the meal. He figured she was probably connecting with her office. Surely, they had protocols for everything that had happened, and Tessa was a rule-follower. She would definitely be doing everything by the book.

He leaned back as he watched the noodles cook, then glanced at her silhouette. If the circumstances were different, he would be enjoying this glimpse into her life as an FBI agent. He'd never gotten such a close look before at either her job or the way she handled herself when she was on the FBI clock. Both were captivating and gave him a new appreciation of her skills and talents. He knew Tessa had a well-earned reputation as a tough but fair FBI agent. She had an excellent track record and was one of the younger agents that had been assigned to the homicide division when she had joined them in the Chicago office. Despite the circumstances, he was finding this experience intriguing.

He finished cooking and slid a steaming plate of the finished concoction toward her, as well as a glass with ice water. Then he got his own plate and drink and sat down across from her at the counter.

"Dinner is served," he announced.

She glanced at the offering, then typed a few more keystrokes, closed the window she had open and turned away from the computer. "Thanks."

"You're welcome. Any news on your partner?"

"Yes. He's doing well. They did have to operate, but it was over quickly and was a simple procedure. He's all stitched up and will be out for the next week or so, depending on how fast he heals up. He'll have to pull some desk duty and do some physical therapy, but he'll be fine. I thought he had broken his collarbone, but thankfully, I was wrong."

She took a bite of her dinner and gave him a small smile—the first smile he had seen on her since this encounter had begun. It warmed him from his head to his toes. Yep, that was the smile he remembered.

"Hey, this is pretty good."

"You sound a bit surprised," he said as he gave her a playful nudge. He thought about the many expressions he had seen her exhibit during their short time together in Atlanta. Most had been severe and filled with anger or frustration, and it was nice to see her relax a little. The driven, determined Tessa was a sight to behold, but this softer side was also attractive, and he knew from experience that she was a thoughtful and giving friend who also was filled with compassion for others. He had missed her so much in his life, yet he also knew it was his own choices that had brought him to this point. Once again, he found himself hoping they could put the past behind them and at least rebuild their friendship as they worked together to stop this criminal enterprise.

Could they start this new normal right now? It was worth a try. "I know I don't have a right to ask, but I really would like to know what's been going on in your life during the last three years." He paused. "Are you seeing anyone?"

She shook her head, and he let out a breath he didn't even realize he'd been holding. He wanted her to be happy, but jealousy swamped him every time he pictured her in the arms of another man.

"No, I don't really date. I don't have the time." She paused. "How about you?" she asked, an eyebrow raised.

"No, no one," he replied. He had gone out with women a couple of times, but nobody was like Tessa. She was simply too unique, a one-of-a-kind treasure, and he'd found that anyone else he dated had never quite measured up. Tessa had set the bar way too high. He took a bite, chewing thoughtfully, then swallowed. "What's been keeping you so busy?"

Tessa shrugged nonchalantly. "After you left, I put all my energy into the job."

Gabe reached over and laid his hand over hers and squeezed it gently. He was pleasantly surprised when she didn't pull away. It was the first real physical contact she had allowed since they had been reintroduced here in Atlanta. "I'm glad God brought you here."

She took a drink with her free hand but still didn't move her other hand that was encased by his. "I remember you never wanted to come with me when I went to church in Chicago. What changed? How did you become a Christian?"

He raised his eyebrows, then furrowed them. "After I witnessed the murder, I was pretty low. I'd seen something horrible and then lost everything, so finally, I started looking up. Have you heard that old adage, you won't know Jesus is all you need until Jesus is all you have? Well, for me, it was easier to do some serious soul-searching when I was stuck in a hotel room day after day with very little contact with the outside world and nothing but fear and foreboding to keep me company. I was so bored one day that I pulled out the Gideon Bible I found in the hotel dresser, and started reading. I finally realized that the money and the possessions I had were never going to make me happy. God guided me to a small group of believers, and I've been growing in my faith ever since."

She smiled, and he thought he saw the same look of peace in her countenance. "I'm glad you introduced me to the idea when we were dating," he said truthfully. "I might not have been so open to welcoming Jesus into my heart if you hadn't planted the seeds."

She turned her hand over and gave his a squeeze, then pulled away. "I'm glad, too." She turned back to the laptop, connected to the surveillance window app and then minimized it and connected to the FBI database. "Ready to go to work? I had to leave the paper file behind at the last safe house, but I can access most of it through our FBI server. We still haven't been able to find out very much about the shooter, but I was wondering if we could talk more about those questionable transactions we asked you about. Do you remember many of the details?"

Gabe sat down beside her at the table, noticing how deftly she had turned the conversation back over to the case. Still, they had made some progress in starting to rebuild the friendship they had once shared, and the black rubber band still hadn't returned to her wrist. He also no longer felt the anger radiating from her that had been hitting him in waves during their first hours together. Yes, they might actually end up as friends again before this was over. But what then?

He didn't even want to think that far into the future. For now, he would be happy with what he had. He said a quick and silent prayer of thanks, then turned his mind to the case, as well.

"Some of them. I do remember the three transactions you mentioned because they were all high-value properties and because BRT was the common buyer."

"Who was your BRT contact?"

"A woman named Sarah Robbins."

Tessa tapped a few keys and a photo of Sarah showed up on the laptop screen. "Is this the woman?"

Gabe glanced at the photo. It showed a woman in her fifties with short dark hair peppered with gray and a winning smile. She looked very professional and sported wire-framed glasses, and she was wearing a navy suit and teal-colored blouse with a choker of pearls. "That's her. She toured the properties with me and then sent over the offer once BRT committed to the purchase. She was my main contact throughout all of the transactions and provided the supporting paperwork and other items I needed to close the deals." He took a drink of water. "She also helped with a purchase located at 513 Hayden Avenue downtown. BRT bought a small restaurant at that address. They said they were going to renovate it and make it into a five-star bistro, but it was a much cheaper property compared to the others. That might be why it didn't make your list."

Tessa added that information to her notes

that she was tapping into a document on the laptop. "Do you remember what bank they used for their financial transactions?"

"Sure, they had several different accounts through Hartfield Savings and Trust." He suddenly snapped his fingers. "I actually know which branch of the bank they usually use. I had to meet Ms. Robbins there a couple of times, and we used their notary to finalize some documents. I also know they preferred cash and rarely trusted internet banking. They told me it was company policy. Sometimes they paid in cash at the bank, and then I took the cash and deposited it directly into Southern Properties' account at our bank." He rubbed his forehead and grimaced. "I should have realized something was up. The cash should have been a red flag, but Ms. Robbins gave me a story about her boss being eccentric, and I bought it hook, line and sinker."

"Were all of the transactions paid in cash?"

"A large portion of each transaction, yes. Sometimes she also gave me two or three checks drawn from different accounts to make up the total purchase price. She explained it away by saying BRT represented different interests, and the properties were going to be owned by portions of different investment companies that they each represented." He tilted his head. "I say a trip to Hartsfield Savings and Trust is in order. Are you up for it?"

Tessa kept typing. "I'm supposed to guard you here at the safe house. We're not supposed to leave."

"So, guard me at the bank," Gabe said as he stood. "It's clear they used that transmitter to follow us to the last safe house, but we're talking about the Ukrainian mafia. They probably have unlimited resources. If they want to find me, they're going to find me. I'm not convinced I'm any safer here than I am out and about in Atlanta." He motioned toward the door. "The banks keep video surveillance recordings of the people who come and go. We need to take a look at those. We might learn a lot about how BRT does business if we can see who comes and goes from that particular branch, and if Sarah sees anyone before or after the meetings we held together."

"We'd have to get a subpoena to get anywhere."

"Not necessarily," Gabe said, hoping to convince her. He was a man of action. The last thing he wanted to do was sit and watch reruns all day while he was being protected at a federal safe house. He'd already done plenty of that when he had been in WIT-SEC awaiting the Montalvo brothers' trial. It nearly drove him crazy. "I have a good relationship with the bank manager, and he would probably let us look at the recordings without one. But if not, you can call and try to get one before we arrive. If we don't see anything unusual or recognize anyone, we can check that box and then move on to the next idea we have. At least we'll be moving forward in the investigation. The bank will probably be eager to assist the federal government to avoid public embarrassment. If you can promise to keep their name out of the papers, they'll probably bend over backward to help."

He could tell she still wasn't convinced. He infused even more enthusiasm into his voice. "Please? Tessa, there must be a reason why BRT and the Ukrainians want me dead. I don't really understand why yet, but maybe it's because I can recognize some of the major players in their money laundering scheme. Shawn's life may in danger this very moment if he isn't already dead. We need to do everything we can to figure out what's going on in this case and as soon as possible before more people get hurt. The clock is ticking."

Tessa leaned back in her chair and looked at Gabe, her expression pensive. Finally, she closed the laptop with a snap. "Okay. Let me call the SAC."

NINE

"Stop! Take a look at that man right there," Gabe said as he motioned toward the screen. The bank security guard quickly paused the recording and they all three leaned closer to the image. "He was a courier for BRT. I don't remember his name, but I do remember his face."

The bank vice president watching the recordings with them checked their file, then nodded. "Yes, that corresponds with a deposit made into one of the BRT accounts at 9:37 a.m. on October 28."

Gabe made a note on a small notepad the bank had provided him. "That's three different BRT couriers, and each is making five or six small deposits in person per month."

Tessa put her hands on her hips. "So that's why there isn't much of an internet trail of their banking habits. They're doing banking the old-fashioned way—with several smaller deposits done in person by various individuals. In-person banking means there is less of a record generated, and the smaller amounts mean no red flags."

The vice president shifted uncomfortably. "Those couriers are also making deposits into multiple bank accounts that we now know are linked to BRT, which is another reason nobody noticed before. We hadn't seen the connection until you showed it to us today."

"I'm going to need a list of each of those accounts that these couriers have accessed."

"Absolutely. But I will need a subpoena to release those records."

Tessa nodded. "Don't worry. You'll have one by this afternoon. And we do appreciate your cooperation. You've been fantastic." She stepped away and made a call to her contact in the Financial Crimes Unit and described what they had found, then started the process to obtain a subpoena. Gabe watched her with fascination. She was the consummate professional, and he loved watching her in action. Her eyes flashed as she described the banking scheme they were just beginning to understand, and the implications of their discovery. She was animated and excited by their progress, and it showed in her demeanor and stance. He thought back over their prior relationship and wasn't even sure he had truly appreciated her and her abilities until the past few days. She was so good. And in his eyes, she grew more and more beautiful with each passing moment.

The bank manager pushed a few buttons on the video monitor, and Gabe turned his attention back to the screen. "Can you get Agent McIntyre close-up pictures of each of these couriers from your video feed?"

"Sure. Give me a couple of minutes." The vice president worked with his security team to get the pictures electronically sent to Tessa's email address, and a few minutes later, Tessa had received them on her phone and had sent them to the Financial Crimes Unit, as well. She shut off her phone and turned back to the vice president and Gabe, who were alternating their attention between Tessa's actions and the bank videos. "The team is already running the identities of each of the couriers and promised to report back to me once they know each of their names and criminal histories, if any."

Tessa and Gabe finished at the bank and headed back to their car. They had made significant progress learning about BRT but still had no idea how everything tied together or why Gabe was being targeted. "Back to the safe house?" Tessa asked as she pushed through the front door of the bank. "We should hear something soon about those couriers."

A bullet shattered the glass on the door she had just opened, coating her with shards of debris. She instantly grabbed Gabe and pushed him back into the bank building, her weapon pulled as she searched for the shooter amongst the nearby buildings and the street surrounding them.

"Are you okay?" she said roughly, still on the lookout for the threat.

"I'm not hit," Gabe responded, astounded that she was once again using her body as a shield to keep him safe. Sure, he was wearing a bulletproof vest, too, but down deep, Gabe knew she would do the same thing whether she was wearing a vest or not. It was in her nature to protect.

A second truth hit him, and all of the positive thoughts he had been thinking about her job suddenly dissipated like a cloud of smoke. He didn't want her hurt. He knew she was often in danger as a field agent, but that fact hadn't really hit home until he had seen it up close and personal. A surge of protectiveness suddenly swept over him. Her own partner had gotten shot just this morning, and Gabe didn't like her being targeted, especially twice in one day. He turned to the bank vice president, and he was unable to keep the frustration from his voice. "Is there another way out of here?"

The vice president's face had paled, and he was trembling from head to toe. He lifted a wary hand and pointed, then started to back away. "That way, down the hall and to the left. There's a back door. A silent alarm will go off when you open it, but I'll call the security company and explain. They're going to need to know about this shooter anyway."

Gabe nodded and then motioned to Tessa who was already on the phone again with her office, reporting the shooting. She finished the call and stowed her phone but still had her Glock in her hand, pointed at the ceiling for safety.

"Stay away from the windows, and wait for the police," she ordered. "They'll be here soon. Until they tell you it's clear, keep everyone inside. Got it?"

The manager nodded, and his hands were

shaking so badly he fisted them and hid them behind his back.

Tessa backed up, then turned and started toward the hallway where the man had pointed. Gabe followed, his eyes darting around as he did so. *Good grief,* he realized fleetingly, *I'm starting to copy Tessa.* They both slipped out the doorway and into the drive-through area, and Gabe was instantly pleased that the roof shielded them from view as they moved around the cars. Despite the adrenaline that was pumping through his veins, having Tessa with him made him feel invincible and strong, even if there was a killer out there aiming for him. It was a dangerous feeling, yet it kept him from totally losing his cool as Tessa followed him into the alley between two of the nearby buildings. He looked right and left but saw no one, and they kept to the side of the alley as they hurried along, hoping that a moving target near the building's walls would be harder to hit. He had no idea where the shooter was but figured the best thing to do was get as far away as possible. Tessa seemed to agree and was following him closely.

"Are you heading somewhere in particular?" Tessa whispered as they ran.

"I know a place close by where we can

hide," Gabe answered. He heard footsteps behind them and a bullet ricocheted off the brick not two feet from his head. It made a whizzing sound as it bounced away and sent a wave of urgency down his spine. He turned to the left and continued running. He heard Tessa stop and fire at their pursuer, but a moment later she was directly behind him again, as if she hadn't paused in the first place.

They passed a large brownstone building and then came to a brick apartment building that had a locked side entrance. The door was a solid slab of metal with no markings and no windows. Gabe pulled his keys from his pocket and quickly found the silver key with a red dot he'd painted on it, unlocked the door and slipped inside with Tessa. He closed the door firmly behind him, verified it was locked then leaned against the wall, trying to catch his breath.

He glanced over at Tessa, who was barely breathing hard, despite their long jaunt from the bank. She raised an eyebrow. "What is this place?"

"Shawn owns an apartment in this building, but few people know about it. He used it for housing clients from out of town and that sort of thing. This is the rear stairwell, and we can get up to the apartment without being seen if we're careful. The building doesn't have cameras or other security."

"Why'd you bring us here?"

Gabe shrugged. "I hoped it would be a safe place to get away from that gunman downstairs. Was it a bad idea?"

Tessa looked around, and he could tell she was studying everything and absorbing details he might not even realize were important, and was also making connections and building her case in her head. Her powers of observation had always been impressive, and she was smart. The strange part was, even though they had only been together again for a couple of days, he was already remembering how to read her expressions and body language. That familiarity was a welcome sense of calm while the storm raged around him.

Tessa finally narrowed her eyes but still didn't respond to his question, and he instantly knew she wasn't pleased to be discover that Shawn had been leading a secret life or that Gabe hadn't mentioned it before now. Apparently, the FBI hadn't known about this particular address.

Why did her expression make him feel guilty? He suddenly felt like he had to defend his friend and coworker. It wasn't his idea to keep an apartment like this, but with everything that had transpired in the past few hours, he had to wonder if Shawn had been using it for illegal and illicit purposes. "Shawn may have made some bad choices, but he wouldn't break the law," he said vehemently.

"So you say," Tessa replied. "How many other secrets did Shawn keep?"

"I wouldn't know. This is the only one I was privy to."

She looked at him carefully as if gauging his truthfulness, then finally released him from her scowl. "And I'm supposed to believe you?"

"Yes, you are."

A beat passed, then another. Finally, she shook her head and motioned toward the interior of the building. "Which apartment?"

"3C." Gabe pushed against the wall and followed the hallway to the back of the apartment complex. Since they had come in through a side entrance, there wasn't much around them except the doors for the first-floor apartments, but they soon came upon a different type of door that led to a stairwell and an elevator next to a stack of built-in mailboxes.

"Let's take the stairs," Tessa said quietly as she opened the stairwell door.

Gabe nodded and followed her, glancing behind him as the door closed, making doubly sure that nobody had followed them. She led with her weapon pulled, her head tilted slightly as she listened for footsteps or any other telltale signs of their pursuer. They reached the third floor without incident and made their way to Shawn's apartment. Gabe gave a silent prayer of thanks that they hadn't come across anyone in the hallway, and he quickly unlocked the door and the two slipped inside.

A horrible smell that vaguely resembled rotten eggs mixed together with burned acetone met them as they closed the door firmly behind them. Tessa wrinkled her nose and glanced over at Gabe. She had smelled death enough times to know what odor had met them at the door, but there was also the stink of burned flesh mixed in, which meant they had probably just stumbled upon another crime scene. She wondered if Gabe could identify the smell and understood what was waiting for them somewhere in the apartment.

"Stay here," she hissed under her breath.

Just because the stench was strong, it didn't mean they were alone in the home. If the perpetrator was still anywhere within the residence, she didn't want to give their presence away. She kept her firearm pointed at the ceiling, but ready if needed, as she began searching the various rooms. She moved silently from area to area, checking even the smallest closet, trying to verify that they were indeed the only ones alive in the apartment.

The body was in the master bedroom, lying on the bed in a mass of ashes and burned bedding. Thankfully the fire that had damaged the corpse was restricted to the mattress and hadn't spread to the other parts of the room. She smelled a faint hint of kerosene mixed in with the other odors and imagined that the fire had probably been started with the flammable liquid. She also saw a discarded fire extinguisher on the floor near the bed, and remnants of fire retardant covered the body and surrounding ashes. The fire had probably been set to hinder the discovery of the identity of the body, but the arsonist had limited the size of the flame so it wouldn't set off any alarms or attract unwanted attention, thus delaying the discovery of the cadaver as long as possible. She glanced at the face, but was unable to tell the identity of the corpse, since someone had burned it beyond recognition. She was fairly certain the body was male, based on the size and shape and the pieces of clothing that were still visible because they hadn't burned completely. The body had been clothed in a men's sports coat that had melted against the skin, and the remains of a pair of men's leather penny loafers were still recognizable, as well. Even the watch, a large men's platinum Rolex, was damaged but remained around the corpse's wrist.

Was it Shawn Parker? The FBI had been searching for him for weeks, and this body had definitely been here awhile. In fact, she was surprised that the smell hadn't started to permeate the nearby apartments. If these were Parker's remains, it would explain why they hadn't been able to locate him and why no one had heard from him in so long. Still, she didn't feel comfortable speculating on the identity without pulling in the medical examiner and the team from the morgue. She quickly finished searching the apartment and then, finding no one, returned to the living room where Gabe was waiting. She paused a moment and listened closely by the front door of the apartment, verifying that whoever was chasing them hadn't discovered their new location. Hearing nothing after several minutes, she turned to Gabe.

"The apartment is clear. Who came up here besides Shawn?"

"The firm used to let new employees stay here sometimes when they first got hired until they could find an apartment of their own, but no one stayed more than a month, and the last time I remember that happening was over two years ago. Then Shawn took over the apartment. As far as I know, he was the only person who ever came here unless he was dating someone who needed a place to stay. That didn't happen very often, but it did occur from time to time. I couldn't tell you the last time he had someone here. He hasn't mentioned this place in quite a while."

"Was he dating anyone recently?"

"Not that I know of, and he would have told me if he'd been seeing someone seriously. We were good friends, and he liked to talk about his girlfriends. I would have heard about it for sure."

"Did Shawn have a Rolex?"

"Yes, a platinum one. Why?"

She absorbed this, then motioned toward the hall that led to the bedrooms. "I'm sorry to say that there's a body in the bedroom, but it's burned so badly I can't tell who it is for sure." She put her hand on his arm and squeezed it, then released it. "There's a good chance it's Shawn Parker. The rest of the apartment is clear." She could see Gabe's face fall at her words, and she sympathized with him. He had already been through a lot over the past couple of days with the shooting at his office and deaths of friends and co-workers, and he had probably just lost another friend. She had been forced to give death notices on several occasions during her career, and to her, it was the worst duty imaginable. It was never easy, and there was no good way to do it. She always knew that, inevitably, she was changing the life forever of the person who was receiving the news. "I'm so sorry for your loss."

"I need to see if it's Shawn," Gabe said quietly as he moved toward the bedroom.

"Okay," she agreed, "but don't touch anything. This entire apartment is a crime scene until we know more."

He stiffened at her words, but she knew he would comply, despite the pain of looking at the corpse of someone who was probably his friend. She followed him in and watched as he swallowed hard at the sight of the body. He turned away for a few moments, then turned back, his hands on his hips and his face grim.

"I think it's Shawn, although with those burns, it's hard to be sure. That looks like his watch on his arm. He had one just like that, and I recognize those shoes. If they're a size ten, it's probably him."

TEN

"I'll be sure to pass that information on to the medical examiner," Tessa responded. Her heart ached for Gabe as she watched the anguish wash over him. Despite their past roller-coaster relationship, it was hard for her to see her former fiancé in so much visible pain. He and the victim had obviously been very close. "I'm going to make some calls from the living room, so you can take a few minutes to regroup if you want to. I'll give you some privacy. Some other agents will be arriving soon to secure the scene, and I need to be here when they arrive, so we have a few minutes before we can head back over to the safe house. Take whatever time you need." She took a step closer but didn't touch him. Every muscle in his body seemed taut to the point of brittleness. "I'm really sorry for your loss, Gabe. I realize he was your friend."

Gabe said nothing for several minutes, then tried to shrug as if he was nonchalant about the discovery, but he failed miserably, and his motion left his body posture defeated and subdued. When he still didn't speak, Tessa put her hand gently on his arm and gave it a soft squeeze. "Are you going to be okay?"

He still didn't answer her for several minutes, but he finally looked up and met her eyes. "Someday. Maybe. I lost so much when I left Chicago, and now, even more is being taken away from me. Shawn had his issues, but he was a good friend. He was my only friend when I first came to Atlanta." He drew his lips into a thin line, and she could tell he was struggling to keep it all together. She stepped closer and gave him a hug, wanting to give him a dash of comfort. Nothing could erase the pain he was feeling, but she hoped her support was at least welcome and helpful. Finally, she pulled back, drew her hand slowly down his cheek, then turned and quietly left the room so he could compose himself. She knew he and Shawn had been business partners as well as friends, and his loss would put a big hole in Gabe's life, regardless of how the case turned out. Even though they suspected that Shawn Parker had been killed, it was quite another thing to have their suspicions confirmed and find his mutilated corpse lying on the bed.

As she returned to the living room, his words resonated even deeper with her, and she mulled them over carefully in her mind. She had never really considered the cost of having someone give up everything so they could enter WITSEC. It was an incredibly high price tag for a person to pay to do the right thing. Any leftover anger she had been feeling toward Gabe withered and died right there. He'd had to make tough choices to go into WITSEC. For the first time, she understood how unfair she had been when she'd directed all of her frustration and antagonism at him after the shooting in his office. Maybe she should have given him a chance to explain sooner. He'd had to make difficult choices, with lifelong consequences, but she had been so focused on herself and her own pain that she hadn't even considered his. The realization was sobering.

She paced restlessly as she phoned in the death they'd discovered and gave the Atlanta team even more details about the attempt on their life at the bank and why they had ended up in Shawn's secret apartment. She was getting tired of being shot at and playing defense. They needed to step up their offense and make some headway in this case, and fast. She hung up with SAC Garcia and made a second call to the Financial Crimes Unit to discuss what they had found at the bank. They confirmed that money paying for the three properties that Gabe had handled came from multiple accounts, and with the bank's help, they were able to trace a lot of the money to two shell companies that were being used to make the purchases along with BRT. Both companies' accounts had been funded with several unusual cash deposits by various couriers who didn't seem to have any other ties to the deposits. The two shell companies in question were Hawks Rise Enterprises, Ltd, and Glenoco. Unfortunately, her team still hadn't learned much about the couriers who were making the cash deposits at the bank or about Sarah Robbins, the contact at BRT who had worked with Gabe on finalizing the sales. She hoped they could discover who was pulling the strings behind these two companies before anyone else had to die. She said a silent prayer asking for comfort for Gabe and protection for them both as they continued the investigation.

* * *

Gabe swallowed, then turned away from the prone body on the bed and the damaged face. His friend's death brought to mind the murder of the man he had witnessed in Chicago that had brought the wave of change to his life, and his chest tightened with the memories. He spun on his heel and left the room, suddenly anxious to be away from the charred remains and the awful smell that was all but suffocating. He didn't go back to the living room, but instead made his way into the guest bedroom that faced the street below. That room had the curtains pulled back from the window frame, and he was able to look down on the wintry scene. It was late afternoon, and the cold kept the Southerners who were more used to ninety-degree temperatures in heavy coats and hats. He had to laugh at them, and his observation was a welcome diversion from his morbid thoughts about Shawn. These people knew nothing about the cold up north. The chilling temperatures here were nothing like what he had experienced in Chicago, but he had been happy about the change and didn't miss the blistering winds or shoveling the snow from his driveway. In fact, there was little he missed about living in

Chicago beyond his relationship with Tessa and his small group of friends.

Gabe's mind returned from his thoughts about Chicago to the here and now. This street was in a fairly affluent part of town, and the neighborhood had gone to great expense to decorate the street and buildings for the upcoming Christmas holiday. Banners with red and green adorned the streetlights, and several Christmas trees were visible through the nearby windows, as well as artistic renditions of snowmen, reindeer and silver bells. Streams of lights, soon to be illuminated once the sun set, were hung over the road. But even with all of the wonderful decorations, it was hard to focus on the holiday and joy that it usually brought when his best friend lay dead in the next room. He was supposed to be thinking about the birth of Jesus, not death. Yet his current situation made it hard to think about anything else.

He returned to the living room where Tessa had just finished another call. She stowed her phone, then pulled on a pair of rubber gloves. "I was going to start looking for clues to see if we could figure out who did this."

"I can't imagine Shawn had any enemies that would murder him, but I guess I'm just naive. I still can't accept that he's involved in something illegal. It's inconceivable." He rubbed his neck absently. "He was my friend. A good friend. How did I miss this?"

Tessa shrugged. "Why don't you tell me about him?"

Gabe thought back to when he had first encountered Shawn. "A few days after I arrived in Atlanta we shared a table at a crowded neighborhood coffee shop, and we hit it off right from the start. By chance we happened to see each other the next day, too, and ended up becoming casual friends over cappuccinos and cinnamon rolls. Coffee morphed into tennis games, and before I knew it, Shawn offered me a position at his real estate firm at a generous starting salary. After only two years and several lucrative deals, I was promoted to partner and was one of the primary movers and shakers in the firm, but it was all because of Shawn. We were like a well-oiled machine, and when the two of us worked together, the deals just came together, almost effortlessly." He shrugged. "The only thing we didn't really agree on was Jesus. Shawn wasn't a believer, and he was still living a rather wild nightlife. On the days when he wanted to party, I went my own way."

Gabe gritted his teeth as the grief overtook him. He looked away, composed himself, then faced her again. "Because we worked so well together, Shawn was able to depend on me to get things done, and then he could spend even more time rainmaking for the company. As a team, we broke several firm sales records, and I received some lucrative bonuses. The money and recognition offered a sense of accomplishment, I guess, and I became a workaholic of sorts, but it was excellent therapy for me and kept me occupied on the good days and the bad. I couldn't be lonely if I worked sixty-hour weeks. The only other place I really ever spent my time outside the office was at my church, where I worked with the youth, but that wasn't as often as I would have liked. I didn't socialize unless it was a firm function, and I never dated." He blew out a breath. "It was just Shawn and me, cranking out the deals."

Tessa came over and stood in front of him, her expression caring. "Did you have a lot of bad days when you first moved to Atlanta?"

"I had my fair share."

"Why?"

"Because I didn't have you."

She stared at him for a few minutes, and

he saw a myriad of emotions flash within her eyes. Finally, she spoke, and her voice was soft, almost like a caress. "Thanks for telling me that. I don't think I ever realized how tough it was on you to have your whole life ripped apart when you went into WIT-SEC. We in law enforcement are so focused on making an arrest and closing our case that I think we forget about the depth of the collateral damage that the witnesses endure." She brushed a stray bunch of hair away from her face and tucked it behind her ear. "I'm guilty of that, at least. In our case, I was so wrapped up in my own pain that I didn't really consider the pain you were in. When I first saw you again, all I felt was anger. I think I've been angry almost every day for the last three years. But I was wrong to feel that way. None of this was your fault. I'm sorry."

Gabe drew her into his arms again, and for several moments, he just enjoyed the comfort and warmth he received in her embrace. "I forgive you. These last few years have been tough on both of us. What matters now is where we go from here." He paused a moment, then asked the question that was burning in his heart. He was grateful he couldn't see her eyes because he was so afraid of rejection. "Do you think we can be friends? Once this whole thing is over, I'd really like to just be together and talk so we can get to know each other again. I realize our relationship has changed and we've both moved on, but it would feel good to reminisce for old times' sake."

"I'd like that," she responded. "Have you learned how to cook?"

He laughed. "Not really," he replied, remembering some of his failed attempts to impress her with his culinary skills. He could ruin a bowl of cereal, if such a thing were even possible. That was one thing they had in common. "I usually just grab a bite when I'm out and about. How about you?"

She shook her head gently. "I haven't either, but I have located the best restaurants in town. You tell me what you want to eat, and I can make a trustworthy recommendation." She stepped back and drew her lips into a thin line. "The first thing we have to do though, is figure out who's trying to kill you and who murdered Shawn. Can you think of anyone who would want to kill him?"

"No. Just like I can't think of anyone who would want to shoot up the firm where I worked. None of this makes any sense to me. All I can imagine is that he is somehow mixed up in the money laundering due to the connections you've uncovered. But I am really having a hard time believing that. Shawn never seemed like a criminal to me. But then what does a criminal act like? It's not like they wear signs around their necks advertising their faults. Still, I thought I was a better judge of character."

"Could you have been so busy that you missed the money laundering?"

He closed his eyes for a moment and sighed, then opened them again and tilted his head slightly. "I guess anything is possible. I was pretty wrapped up in my own projects, and even though I was a partner, I didn't see any sign of wrongdoing, but honestly, I wasn't looking for it, either."

"I wonder if you know something without realizing its importance." She bit her bottom lip as she seemed to ponder the possibilities. Gabe doubted she even knew she was doing it. Her gesture made him want to touch her bottom lip and smooth it with his finger. "Maybe one or more of these deals you did with Shawn were the crux of the money laundering. You must know something the Ukrainians don't want you to share. We just have to keep looking until we find it."

ELEVEN

"The man who hired the gunman, Adrien Metzger, to do the shooting at Southern Properties, was Maxim Balanchuk. We don't know much about Mr. Balanchuk yet, but the FBI was finally able to trace a payment back to his bank account in Ukraine. I've heard back from INTERPOL but he's not popping up in any of their systems. So far, all I've been able to find is a record from about ten years ago where he was caught stealing a car with a friend. Before you ask, the friend isn't popping up in the system, either." Tessa's colleague's voice was filled with frustration as she reported on the latest intelligence updates from the office. Details about the gunman and his boss were proving to be more elusive than she'd expected.

"He has no known associates and no other criminal record that I've come across. We also can't find a current address for him anywhere," the agent continued. "I think our initial assessment was correct. Balanchuk works for the Ukrainian mob, and Metzger was a simple gun for hire who must have lied about his ability to handle explosives. He was supposed to go into that office and reset the bomb, but instead, he went in there shooting as many people as possible, hoping that if he didn't manage to set the bomb correctly, he could still reach the end objective of putting the company out of business and keeping the focus away from the business transactions."

"Okay." Tessa nodded. "But maybe we can learn about the shooter and his boss in a different way. Can you run the building's security video feeds back a couple of days and see if you catch anyone doing surveillance of the building in the days before the attack? Maybe we'll see the gunman do something or learn something else about them that can take our investigation in a new direction."

"Sure, we'll start today," the FBI agent replied.

"Thanks for the update." Tessa hung up, leaned back in her chair and slowly put her phone back on the table. They were back in the safe house, but Tessa felt anything but calm and relaxed. Before this latest call from one of her contacts at the FBI office, her boss, SAC Garcia, had given her another update, but none of the news was good. They still hadn't been able to discover the identity of the gunman at the FBI building who had taken shots at them in the parking lot. The person had even cleaned up the brass after taking the shots and then had apparently disappeared into the wind. They had made a small amount of progress with the killer Tessa had shot that had fired at Chris in the safe house. At least now they knew his name and nationality, which was Ukrainian, but they hadn't found much else, despite their many inquiries with international agencies. INTERPOL was normally a great resource, and they had a history of cooperation between the two agencies that went back years, but INTERPOL couldn't give them what they didn't have. The connection with Ukraine was growing, but where were these mercenaries coming from? This man Tessa had killed apparently had no internet footprint, and facial recognition software hadn't found a single match in any of the usual databases. Was he a local boy or also a European? How did all of the pieces fit together?

Gabe walked into the kitchen carrying an empty cereal bowl and stopped when he saw Tessa's face. "You've looked happier."

"I've been happier." She sighed. "We still know next to nothing about the men that have been using us for target practice. Apparently, there is an endless supply of nameless, face-less mercenaries available for hire in Eastern Europe. The only connection we've found so far is that they all like to eat Lviv chocolate. Both the shooter at your office and the one I took down at the safe house had some in their pockets. The Lviv Chocolate Factory is a one-of-a-kind enterprise in the country and is a well-known favorite of the locals." She rubbed her hands together. "My boss was also not happy about you getting shot at again. She and I both are really worried about that large target on your back."

"At least we made a lot of progress on the case."

"Even so, it's a high price to pay if you take a bullet in the process."

"Did she have any good news to report?"

"Yes, she said Chris is doing well. The doc-tors are pleased with his improvement, and they all agree he's going to make a full re-covery."

"Well, that's something, but I'm afraid you're not going to like what I'm about to tell you."

She raised an eyebrow as Gabe took a seat across from her at the kitchen table. "Oh?"

"I've been doing some research on the laptop you're letting me use—digging into those two companies that were behind all of those accounts at the bank that were used to buy the properties I sold to BRT. You know—Hawks Rise Enterprises, Ltd, and Glenoco."

Tessa leaned forward. "Find anything interesting?"

"Yep," he said, his tone soft and enticing. He could be talking about something as dry as the weather or the latest golf scores and she would still be mesmerized by that voice. It made her feel warm inside, despite the feelings of self-doubt that still plagued her when he looked at her. "These two legal business entities only exist on paper. They don't perform any legitimate economic function."

"Both of them?"

"Yes. Both of them. They define the words 'shell company.' But they have a variety of income and expenditures on their reports that are not well explained. In short, their numbers don't add up."

"How did you get so good at doing research on the internet?"

"Practice," he said with a shrug. "Mostly, I wanted to know what the Montalvos were up to and how I could stay safe, so I started learning as much as I could, but I'm no pro. I know just enough to be dangerous." He grimaced. "I also discovered something else. It looks like both companies are receiving additional income through cryptocurrencies and the dark web."

"That's impressive," Tessa replied. "I don't know much about the dark web, but I do know that Bitcoin and other cryptocurrencies like that aren't subject to the same regulatory requirements as normal currency banking. That suggests to me that this case is even bigger than I thought."

"That's right," Gabe agreed. "Companies using cryptocurrencies also can operate internationally, beyond the reach of government financial regulators, and they leave little to no paper trail. You said yourself you thought the money laundering through the real estate purchases at Southern Properties was just the tip of the iceberg, and you were right. Cryptocurrencies are a great way to wash dirty money. Whatever we've stumbled across here is big, and very dangerous."

"Can you do research on the dark web?"

Gabe shook his head. "Not well enough to find what we want. I think we need an expert to dig even deeper, and I've reached the end of my skill level. We need a true hacker." He tilted his head and gave her a smile—the kind that used to melt her insides. "Know anyone that can help us out?"

"I don't personally, but I know someone who might." She pulled out the laptop and opened the encrypted FBI program. A few moments later, it was making a ringing tone just like the old-fashioned phones. Then a young African American man's face appeared on the screen. Behind him, she could see a board for Blokus, a game they played from time to time when they had the chance, on the counter.

"Tessa! It's your move. Are you ready? Even though you have no hope of beating me, I've got your number."

Tessa laughed. "I can't play right now, Evan. I'm actually calling about work."

Gabe raised an eyebrow at the game reference but she ignored him. Instead she focused on the smiling face of her friend, a tech genius who lived up in Chicago. He practically lived in his basement that was filled with gadgets and old computer equipment, much like Jerome at the FBI technology department, but she couldn't fault the results. Evan Kemp was her go-to friend when she had a tech question she couldn't wrap her head around that might not be quite legal. Also, like Jerome, he was a mastermind behind the keyboard, despite his unkempt appearance and thoroughly messy workspace.

"Evan, I need to pick your brain about the dark web."

"Go ahead." He took a bite of pizza from a piece that looked like it had been sitting by his computer for quite some time. Tessa grimaced internally but kept the smile on her face.

Evan chewed and swallowed. "It's not my forte and I don't use it much, but I have friends who can probably help."

"We need someone who can answer some questions for us about cryptocurrency transactions, but we prefer a local who might know some of the regional players. We also need a person who knows about the international side of things. The case we're working on might have ties to Ukraine in particular. I'm in Atlanta. Got anyone in mind?"

Evan took a moment to think, then hit a few keys. "Sure. I know a guy who's young and just getting started who was bragging about how he had recently made the big time with one of his programs. He was all excited because he thought now he was going to make a heap of cash and could marry his sweetheart and live happily ever after. Name and address coming at you. Tell him I sent you, okay? He's an old friend."

"Will do. I'll get back to the game soon. I promise."

Evan smiled and pointed at her. "I'm holding you to that. You won't win, but I'm willing to give you a fighting chance." He winked at her, and then the screen flickered and the app closed, leaving them back on the desktop screen.

"You play games over the internet?" Gabe's voice broke into her train of thought, and she closed the laptop with a snap.

"Yes. Evan and I have been friends for a while. I actually arrested him when he was in high school up in Chicago, but he's a good kid who just made some mistakes, and he's back on the right track now. He's a board game fanatic, and even though he's the most skilled hacker I know, he won't play computer games. We've played a few different board games over the internet together since I met him, all using video programs. It's been a good way to connect and check up on him. His family is a living nightmare, so I'm trying to keep him on the straight and narrow as he finds his way."

"I like that. I've been doing some activities with the youth at my church. They're challenging but keep me jumping. I'm hoping to make the same kind of difference in a few of their lives, as well." He motioned toward the front door. "Can we go meet this contact Evan gave us, or will your boss nix it?"

Tessa shrugged. "All I can do is try." She grabbed her phone, but Gabe touched her gently before she made the call.

"I heard a rumor that you were up for promotion in a few months. Any truth to that?"

Tessa smiled and tilted her head slightly. "Now, where did you hear that?"

"Is it true?"

Tessa looked at him strangely but finally nodded. The source probably didn't matter, in the grand scheme of things. "It's true. My boss is retiring in three months or so. I'm being groomed to assume her position when she leaves. It's a great opportunity."

"I'm proud of you, Tessa. That's exciting news. So, if all goes as planned, you'll be the head of the Chicago office?"

"That's right, and thank you," she said with a smile. His praise warmed her all over and, suddenly, the air felt thick and hard to breathe. She looked into his eyes and saw genuine pride reflected back at her. It was mesmerizing. Had his eyes always been that blue?

A moment passed, then another, as they just stood there, gazing into each other's eyes.

Finally, she snapped out of it and her brain started working again. She was no teenager in love. Why was she acting like one? Besides, she wasn't any good at personal relationships. That had become more than evident. The people who claimed to love her all seemed to disappear from her life. She quickly looked away and took a few steps toward the front door. "Ah, sorry. I'd better make that call."

She called Garcia and described their plans and was pleasantly surprised when Garcia approved the move. She hung up and turned to Gabe. "We're good to go. The contact's name is Mitch Jacobs, and since he isn't directly related to the case, Garcia thinks the odds of you becoming a target again when we head over to see him are pretty low."

"Let's hope she's right." Gabe grabbed his jacket. "Hopefully we'll discover something new."

Tessa followed him out the door but suddenly felt awkward and unsure. Was she still attracted to Gabe? She hadn't expected the feelings she had just experienced, but she couldn't deny them either, and she was honest enough with herself to admit they existed, even though they were a surprise.

Trepidation mixed with a strange longing that she thought she had eliminated from her life. Did she want to renew her relationship with Gabe? Was it worth the risk of another broken heart?

Mitch Jacobs lived in an old apartment complex in one of the seedier parts of town. A group of teenagers were hanging around near the doorway to the six-story brick building, and they were passing around cigarettes and laughing as they made fun of the passing motorists. Most were wearing jeans and coats with several pockets adorned with gang colors, and they were scruffy and had a threatening appearance despite their youth. Three or four of them leaned casually against the bricks and stood as if they were going to challenge the newcomers as they approached, but as Tessa and Gabe neared, Tessa moved her jacket so they could see the badge on her belt, and the teens were quick to turn and hurry away in the opposite direction without a confrontation. Gabe was secretly glad the teenagers weren't up for a fight. Protectiveness had surged within him as the young men had eyed Tessa, and he'd wondered for a moment or two if they'd even be able to make it into the building without a serious problem.

The road had a few older-model cars parked on both sides of the street, but beyond the youth who had basically disappeared after a few minutes, there were no other pedestrians milling around. The ground was dirty and littered with trash, and a foul smell was emanating from somewhere nearby, but they ignored their surroundings and entered the front door of the building. A drunk in a dark coat was lying in the corner of the foyer emanating a new and potent odor, but since he was snoring and not hurt or in trouble, they let him be and proceeded up the stairs. Mitch's apartment was on the fourth floor, and once they found the right door, they knocked and stepped back.

Gabriel wrinkled his nose. "Do you smell that?" It was a sour smell like rotting fruit that made it hard to breathe.

"Yeah, I smell it, and that's a different stench than what we were getting downstairs," Tessa said under her breath. "Recognize the odor from your friend's apartment?"

Gabe raised an eyebrow. "Do you think we just discovered another body?"

"It's certainly possible."

She banged on the door a second time. "FBI! Open up!"

They both listened intently, but neither heard any sounds coming from inside the apartment. Then they heard a soft sound. "Did you hear that whimper? It sounded like a child or someone that's hurt."

Gabe nodded. He'd also heard a noise. Someone or something was in the apartment, and whatever it was sounded injured or afraid. "I did. We need to get in there."

"I agree. Sounds like exigent circumstances to me."

She knocked one last time, and when she still didn't get any response, she motioned for Gabe to move out of the way, then leaned back, pulled her weapon and kicked the door open. The wood splintered at the force of the blow along the door frame by the lock, and she pushed it a second time with her foot and it swung open with a squeak and a groan.

Gabe raised an eyebrow and reminded himself to stay out of Tessa's way if she was ever motivated to go somewhere. The woman was one tough lady. She entered carefully, once again calling out that she was law enforcement, and pointed her gun at the ceiling, ready to face whatever threat she found.

Gabe did his best to stay out of her way, then followed her into the small, dingy apartment. He wrinkled his nose as the smell got even worse the farther they went past the threshold. Thankfully, there was no smell of fire added to the mix this time, but it was clearly the scent of death, combined with other offending smells, and it was all he could do not to gag as he followed carefully behind Tessa. He watched for threats but was also careful not to impact the potential crime scene in any way.

Mitch Jacobs was sitting in his living room at a computer desk, slumped in his chair. A small bullet hole marred the side of his head, and blood trickled down his neck. The skin was mottled and blue, clearly showing signs of death. There would be no happily-ever-after for him.

TWELVE

Gabe found himself staring at Mitch's body, shocked at the sight of another dead person less than twenty-four hours later. It was obvious that the corpse had been there for a while, and the smell seemed to have permeated everything within the apartment. Thankfully, this person wasn't decimated like the last, but the stench made Gabe's stomach turn and he squeezed his nose, then tried to block the odor with his sleeve. Unfortunately, nothing helped.

After snapping on a pair of rubber gloves and confirming that the victim was obviously dead, Tessa proceeded to search the rest of the small apartment, her gun pulled and ready. She quickly checked each room, just in case the murderer was still hiding somewhere.

Gabe watched her work but felt confident the killer had fled after ending Mitch's life.

He glanced uncomfortably around the apartment, but his gaze continually returned to the sight of the poor victim. He hadn't been friends with Mitch like he had known Shawn, yet the death still affected him greatly. The young man appeared to be in his early twenties, with dark, shaggy hair and pimples marring his skin. He wore old, navy blue sweatpants, a faded burgundy T-shirt and a gray zippered hoodie that probably hadn't seen a washing machine in months. The victim had obviously not been expecting to die since he still had an expression of surprise frozen into his features. It was hard to stomach, and pity swept over Gabe and left him feeling empty inside. One of Mitch's hands had dropped by his side, but the other was still lying motionless on the computer keyboard, as if he were about to strike a key at any moment. Had he been playing a game when he'd taken his last breath, or sending a message to his girlfriend?

So much potential, now wasted forever.

Tessa returned a short time later, her weapon stowed, and Gabe turned his attention back to her. "The apartment is clear," she said in a matter-of-fact tone as he met her eyes. She shivered at the lack of heat in the apartment and rubbed her arms absently. "I wonder what we heard through the door?"

They both stood silently for a minute, and then Gabe raised his index finger and pointed under the desk. "I think I know where that sound is coming from. Do you have another pair of gloves with you?"

She nodded and handed him a pair, and he snapped them on, then crouched by the desk. Careful not to touch the body, Gabe reached under the wood and came back with a small puppy that had been huddling under some old dirty clothing at the dead man's feet. The animal whimpered as Gabe picked him up and moved placidly in his hands, as if it lacked the strength to be more active. It was a small mixed-breed dog, with soft, short hair about an inch long all over that was a mottled mixture of browns, black and white. The animal whined again and licked Gabe's gloved hand.

Tessa's eyes softened when she saw the small animal, and she reached out to touch the matted fur. "Poor thing. He's probably been cowering under there since it happened, and who knows how long he's been without food and water. Want to check the kitchen and see if you can find him something to eat and drink? Just try not to disturb the crime scene."

"Sure." He held the dog close and moved toward the small kitchen. There were bowls on the floor that looked like they had once held food and water for the animal, but now they were both empty and dry, and Gabe was amazed the animal had survived. His master has obviously been dead for several days. He quickly picked up the bowl and filled it from the spigot at the sink, then found a bag of dry kibble and filled the remaining bowl.

The puppy drank thirstily from the bowl and promptly threw up all over the floor. Gabe was cognizant of the fact that the dog was messing up a crime scene against Tessa's explicit instructions, but right now, the life of the dog came first. He gently soothed the animal, then cleaned up the mess with paper towels he found on the counter and shoved them all in a plastic grocery bag so they wouldn't contaminate whatever clues, if any, that might be in the trash can or elsewhere. A few minutes later, the dog's stomach had settled some and it once again tried to drink a little. Gabe found a small bit of cheddar cheese in the refrigerator and fed that to the dog in small, bite-size pieces. He wished he knew more about dogs, but he'd never been around them much and wasn't sure exactly what to do.

The dog greedily gulped down the cheese and also ate a few pieces of the dry food, once Gabe had checked it to make sure it wasn't moldy. He didn't want the puppy to eat too fast and throw up again, so after the animal had gotten a small amount to eat, he picked the dog up and gave it a thorough examination, taking it away from the food still left in the bowl. Although the dog was dirty and smelled rather badly, he didn't find any obvious injuries or any fleas or other bugs. He got another paper towel, wet it and tried to clean the puppy as much as he could, then he took another paper towel and dried the soft fur. It didn't clean the dog completely, but it helped eliminate some of the smell. After about half an hour had passed, he carried the pup back into the living room where Tessa had welcomed the crime scene team that had just arrived and was explaining what they had found in the house. She introduced them all around, then continued where she had left off about the case. When she finished talking to her colleagues, she turned to Gabe and gave the pup a friendly pat on the head.

"That pup looks a lot happier now," Tessa observed.

"She's a girl—a terrier mix, if I had to guess," Gabe said with a smile. "She probably weighs around eight or ten pounds and is about four months old. I found a note on the refrigerator that said she was due for her next shots, so that's how I know her age." He gave the dog a gentle rub on her neck. "I think she was starving, but I gave her some water and cheese, and a little bit of dog food, and she started to pep up." He held her up so Tessa could get a good look. "Her name is Kona, according to her collar."

"What a cutie!" Tessa said as she scratched the dog's head playfully. Kona responded by trying to lick her fingers and scrambling to get closer to Tessa, despite Gabe's hold.

"Wow, she really likes you," Gabe noticed.

Tessa's brow furrowed. "Don't even think about it. I have no room in my life for a dog."

Gabe raised his eyebrow, wondering if that's how she felt about him, too. He could even hear her voice the same words in his mind. *I have no room in my life for you.*

But did he want her to make room for him again? His answer to that question seemed to change almost hourly. He was definitely still attracted to her, but was he ready to pursue her again, knowing there was a better-than-average chance of failure? She had just confirmed that she was next in line for a powerful job that would be both high-pressure and time-consuming. Would she want a relationship on top of all that? He rubbed the dog absently as he considered his options, then jumped as Tessa broke his train of thought and pointed to a picture on the desk. It was a photo of the decedent and a girl with black hair and pretty gray eyes. They were both smiling and tangled in an amorous embrace with mountains in the background and a row of canna lilies in the foreground that had just started to bloom.

"Looks like Mitch had a girlfriend." She reached for the photo, apparently oblivious to Gabe's well-hidden thoughts and emotions, and set it flat on the desk's surface to remove the glare. Then she pulled out her phone and took a picture of the photo and sent it to her team. "I'll get them to run her face through facial recognition, but please look around and see if you find any clues about her name or contact information. She might be our best way of discovering what happened here." She finished the message to the FBI and hit

Send, then continued looking through the desk, while Gabe walked around the apartment, taking in the furnishings. Mitch Jacobs had obviously not been living the high life, and his furniture was a collection of garage sale pieces that were mismatched and in different levels of disrepair. His couch was a dark green color that had gone out of style years ago and had visible lumps in most of the cushions. In the bedroom the mattresses rested on the floor without a frame, and his dresser was chipped and cluttered. He had only two pictures on his wall—both of '80s rock and roll bands. Not seeing anything of interest, Gabe returned to the living room and looked around Mitch's desk. The wood was cracked and littered with dirty dishes, a game console and several old magazines and comic books. One thing, however, was conspicuously absent, and he turned to Tessa, who had been searching the drawers.

"His computer tower is missing," they said together.

One of the crime scene techs, an older balding man with an infectious grin, gave Tessa a friendly nudge. "You guys are finishing each other's sentences?"

Tessa elbowed his chest in a brotherly fashion. "Back off, Carl, or you'll get stuck with the bill for the next pizza night."

"I'm just sayin'…" he continued with a wink.

Tessa frowned, but her expression was lighthearted and playful. "The last bill topped a hundred bucks, Carl. Tread carefully."

Carl held up his hands in mock surrender and returned his focus to the job at hand. "Fine, fine. I hear you, but I call them like I see them."

"He might have been working on something when he was killed—something the murderer didn't want us to find," Gabe said, trying to shift the subject back to the matter at hand. He didn't think he was jealous, especially since the tech was old enough to be Tessa's father. And their exchange *had* been more friendly than romantic. But feelings of protectiveness and, yes, jealousy, has sprung up within his chest. He tried to push them away and focus on the case. "Or maybe the attacker didn't know much about computers, so he took the entire tower just to cover his bases."

Tessa turned from Carl and nodded. "Yes, that's probably what happened. You're getting a real knack for this!" Her phone chirped, and she answered and stepped away to hold the conversation with the caller. A few minutes later, she was back. "We have a name and address for the girlfriend. Let's go."

"That was fast," Gabe observed. He held up Kona, who whimpered and licked his thumb. "What about the dog?"

Tessa looked over at Carl, who shook his head vehemently. "Don't leave him with us. We've got enough to do."

She rolled her eyes, but relented. "Okay, fine. Bring her along and we'll figure it out later. I want to find this girlfriend before she disappears or gets killed, as well."

It was already dark as they made their way back to the car, and Tessa watched as Gabe let the small puppy snuggle close against his chest between his shirt and his jacket. He didn't seem to mind the smell, and even Tessa was getting used to it as they got in and started the drive over to the girlfriend's apartment. She was glad Gabe had fed and cleaned up the poor animal the best he could, and she hoped it didn't suffer any long-term effects from the neglect it had sustained. She wasn't sure what they were going to do with the dog, but right now, her focus was entirely on Mitch's girlfriend. "The woman's name is Kristy Hartfield. She lives alone and is single with no kids. She's a preschool teacher and lives about ten minutes away," Tessa supplied.

"I hope the neighborhood where she lives is better than this one," Gabe said as he glanced around the street. "I would worry about a woman living alone in this area." He shifted and stepped over a broken beer bottle. "Actually, I'd worry about *anyone* living alone in this district." His voice was smooth and calm like a radio disc jockey's again, and the tone sent a warmth through Tessa that spread comfortably along her spine. She felt peaceful and secure, despite having just dealt with another death.

"This area has a history of drugs and crime, that's for sure," Tessa agreed, trying to focus on anything but the feelings he was evoking. "I guess Mitch didn't have much choice. From what Evan said in his text, Mitch made most of his money by running scams on the dark net. He was quite the computer genius but also spent a lot of time gaming, which seriously cut into his income potential. Still, Evan claimed Mitch was doing some work on an international scale, so maybe Mitch's fortunes were about to change."

"Or maybe that's why he was killed," Gabe suggested.

A silence fell between them as she drove, and the streetlights, mixed with the occasional Christmas lights, gave her an almost relaxed feeling for the first time since this Gabe had returned into her life. The air between them felt magnetized the longer she spent behind the wheel, however, and even though he said nothing, her skin began to prickle with electricity just by being close to him. She had felt this way a lot when they had been dating, as if the attraction between the two of them was almost palpable. Now she wasn't so sure how she felt about it. She couldn't deny his return to her life had been a balm to her ego. Yet she was still scared to trust him and the emotions he was beginning to evoke in her. Thankfully, the drive was short, and she fled the car as soon as she parked, eager for the feelings to dissipate.

The one-story building was small and constructed with red brick that had been popular in the 1970s, and had two identical mirrored sides, each with a black-door next to a small four-paned window.

Tessa knocked on Ms. Hartfield's door and took a step back, just as Gabe approached and stood by her side. She glanced at him furtively, but his expression was neutral. If he was feeling the same attraction she was, he sure wasn't showing it. Had it all been in her head? Had she imagined the goose bumps that had run up and down her arms? She sighed and pushed the questions aside so she could focus on the job at hand. With a deep breath, she turned back toward the door and announced her presence. "FBI. Open up."

She heard footsteps and a knocking sound inside, as if someone was quickly gathering items and trying to run away. She met Gabe's eyes as she pulled her weapon. "Please stay here and shout if she tries to go out this door. I'm heading for the back."

He nodded in agreement, but before he could even reply, she had turned and was heading toward the rear of the duplex. She stepped carefully around the lattice-covered trash can and continued along the side of the building. Still hearing noises inside, she kept her Glock 9 mm handgun pointed toward the sky. A cat startled her as it made a noise and then ran off into the night, but she ignored it and kept her back against the wall as she proceeded. A door slammed, and she heard feet shuffling along the ground. She took a breath, then rounded the corner of the building into the backyard, her gun now pointed straight at the woman who had just emerged through the back door of the duplex and who was carrying a laptop and dragging a small green suitcase behind her.

"Freeze!"

The woman did so and was so surprised to see Tessa that she dropped both the laptop computer and the handle to the suitcase at the same time. Both crashed to the ground as the woman started shaking uncontrollably. She put her hands up in a position of surrender and fat, shiny tears started streaming down her face.

"Don't kill me!" she pled, her voice near hysterics.

Kristy Hartfield stood trembling before her.

THIRTEEN

"I can't believe he's dead," Kristy said softly, her eyes red-rimmed and puffy from crying. "Are you absolutely sure?"

Tessa nodded. "We're sure. I'm so sorry for your loss." She hardly recognized Kristy from the driver's license photo she had been sent on her phone, or the photo they had seen in Mitch's apartment. Instead of black hair, this woman before them was now a blonde, and she was wearing quite a bit of makeup that disguised her pimply skin. Her eyes were heavily painted with blue shadow, and her lipstick was a fire-engine red. Black mascara now streaked down her cheeks where the makeup had become a casualty of her tears. Skintight faux-leather pants clung to her body, as well as a sequined Christmas sweater that depicted the Grinch from the Dr. Seuss television special. The makeup made it hard to determine her age from her appearance, but according to the Georgia Department of Motor Vehicles, she was twenty-two years old. She had come back in the house at Tessa's command and was now sitting at the kitchen table next to a box of tissue, and had already gone through a good number of them as Tessa had explained why they were there.

"I knew something had to be wrong. I just knew it. I had this feeling, you know?" She sniffled and blew her nose again.

"I'm so sorry," Tessa repeated. "I know this is difficult, but do you think you can answer a few questions for us? We want to find out who did this to Mitch, so anything you can tell us about him would be helpful, even if you don't think it's important."

Kristy rubbed her eyes, which only made them redder. "What I know is that he wouldn't want me talking to the FBI."

Gabe had been leaning against the front door, blocking it with his body, yet standing casually in a nonthreatening stance. He shifted, and Kona gave a small whimper as she was jostled under his jacket.

Kristy noticed, and her attention went instantly to the small bump nestled against Gabe's chest. "Is that Mitch's dog?" She stood and moved in front of Gabe in two quick steps, trying to get a better look.

Tessa tightened her jaw impatiently, but Gabe smiled at Kristy, who was instantly charmed, and pulled out the puppy from beneath his jacket. "Yes. We found her under his desk."

"Kona!" she cried, obviously familiar with the small animal. Kona yelped happily as she recognized Kristy, and she whimpered and scrambled to get out of Gabe's hold and into Kristy's arms. Gabe released her, and the dog started licking Kristy's face as soon as she was close enough. Kristy laughed happily and hugged the dog close. It was obvious they were friends.

"I take it you know the dog," Tessa said with a smile.

"Sure, I do. I'm the one who gave her to Mitch. She was his birthday present last month. I thought maybe if he had to take the dog out sometimes, and had someone else to think about, he'd finally start leaving his apartment once in a while and get some fresh air. That man could stay behind his keyboard for weeks at a time and never see the light of day. I'm lucky he even stopped to eat."

"I know the type." Tessa leaned back in

her chair. "We know Mitch was doing some work on the dark web before he died. What we need to know is who he was working for. Do you have any ideas?"

Kristy instantly sobered and instead of releasing her cuddled the dog close to her stomach. "I still don't think Mitch would like me talking to you."

"That may have been true when he was alive, but don't you think he'd want you to help us find out who did this to him? We're on his side, Kristy. We want justice for Mitch."

Kristy appeared to be considering Tessa's words, then finally made her decision. "Okay. But if I tell you, I'll need your help. The man he works for is vicious. He'll kill me if he thinks I've told you anything, just like he killed Mitch. That's why I was afraid to go over there and even check on the dog." She scratched Kona's neck absently. "I've been calling Mitch for over two weeks and haven't heard back from him. That's not like Mitch. I mean, there would be times that he was so wrapped up in a game that I wouldn't hear from him for a couple of days, but eventually he would at least send me a text or two. This time, I didn't hear from him at all, but I was so scared I didn't want to chance going out. I've been too terrified to even leave my apartment."

"We can protect you. You have my word," Tessa said vehemently. "If you help us identify his killer, we can make sure you're safe."

Kristy continued to stroke the small dog as she talked, which obviously made her feel more comfortable and at ease. Her voice trembled as she began but got stronger as she continued with her story. "Mitch was always more interested in his games than in actually making money, and he spent most of his time playing online. He was good on the dark web too, and he ran the occasional scam to pay his rent and buy food, but his main love was the games. He was hoping to develop his own game and make a fortune with it. Then this guy approached him and offered him a deal to create a game just for him with very detailed specifications and requirements. The man was going to pay him a crazy amount to do so, and the game was only available on the dark web to a few particular players. The participants were handpicked and used the game to transfer huge amounts of cryptocurrency. At first Mitch thought all the money was fake and just part of the game, but then he realized that it wasn't a game at all, but real. Then he discovered that the man was using his game to do some illegal things. Mitch got scared when he saw what was happening, and he realized he was in too deep, but by that time, the man said if Mitch ever tried to stop working for him, he would kill him."

"Do you know what kind of illegal things the game could do?" Gabe asked.

Kristy shook her head. "Mitch never said, and I didn't ask. The whole thing scared me."

"What do you know about the game?" Tessa asked. "Can you describe it?"

"I don't really know that much about it, even though Mitch tried to get me interested. When he talked about it, it was almost like he was speaking a foreign language." She shrugged and continued patting the dog. "I do remember that he said he designed it almost like a combination of those old games Risk and Stratego, but then added buying and selling and an economic side to the warfare parts of it, kind of like Monopoly. He said the players were supposed to build a kingdom by moving their armies around and claiming territories, and along the way, they could earn prizes and purchase weapons and all sorts of things to make them more powerful. A lot of the game also seemed to be about buying property, like beach houses and other high-priced items like airplanes and yachts. Mitch had to deal with the players a lot, but he had some trouble understanding them because they seemed to be from Eastern Europe and sometimes their English wasn't very good. He complained a lot about that, actually." She frowned, then continued. "To be honest, gaming isn't my thing, so I didn't pay that much attention when he tried to show me more about the actual program." She reached for another tissue, and her eyes teared up again as she spoke. "I loved Mitch Jacobs, but sometimes, I really didn't understand him or the work he did."

"Do you know the man's name who Mitch was working for?" Tessa asked hopefully.

"He said his name was Bryce Cameron. Mitch met with him a couple of times face-to-face here in Atlanta and said he was surprised by how smart the guy was about money and economic things. He ran some sort of international business. Mitch called him BC for short."

A chill went down Gabe's back as he heard his enemy's name. He didn't remember the name Bryce Cameron from any of his real estate transactions, but that had to be the man who had been trying to kill him for the past few days. It was the only thing that made sense.

But why kill him? Because he had been involved in several of the real estate transactions that had been used to launder Bryce's dirty money? They still didn't have proof of that, but they were getting closer every minute to discovering the truth.

"What's on the computer?" Gabe asked softly, pouring on the charm. He could tell his voice was affecting her, and although he rarely used his smooth-talking tones to encourage someone, he felt that now was an appropriate time to use every weapon at his disposal to find out what was going on.

"That's Mitch's laptop. He used it when he was visiting over here and didn't want to drive back and forth," Kristy replied, giving him a smile along with the explanation.

"Do you think we could borrow it?" Gabe asked. "We promise to return it to you once this case is over."

Kristy seemed hesitant, so Gabe kept talking, using his most dulcet timbre. "I know it's special to you, and you'll want to keep it as a reminder of your relationship with Mitch, but we might find something on it that can help us solve this case and find Mitch's murderer."

She finally succumbed, just as Gabe could see Tessa rolling her eyes from her position behind the young teacher. He smiled inwardly, knowing he would get teased about this event not too far into the near future. "I guess you can take it. As long as I get it back. I don't even know if it got damaged or not when I dropped it. Anything is possible."

"You'll get it back," Tessa interjected, cutting to the chase. It was easy for Gabe to see that her patience was wearing thin. "And even if the drop damaged the computer some, our techs can still do a lot with the hard drive." She picked up the computer from the sand-colored Formica kitchen table. "Do you know the name of the game Mitch created?"

"Sure. It was called *Excelsior*. It's Latin. It means 'ever upward,' or something like that."

Tessa and Gabe talked a bit more with Kristy about witness protection, but Kristy ended up deciding her best bet was to go visit her sister in Virginia. Since the MARTA train station was just down the street from Kristy's duplex, she even opted to go there on her own without any FBI escort. She claimed she knew many of the people in the neighborhood and didn't want anyone seeing her talking to law enforcement or doing anything out of her normal routine that seemed suspicious. She asked if she could take Kona with her, so a few minutes later, she was on her way, pulling the suitcase behind her again, but this time carrying the small dog in the crook of her arm.

Tessa and Gabe watched her go and verified that she entered the MARTA station, then they returned to their car and headed back to the safe house once again. Tessa had already called in the name Bryce Cameron to her team, and Gabe knew the FBI was probably already frenetically searching for the man and anything else they could find out about him before anyone else was killed. Tessa had also told him the rest of the plans for the evening. Another agent would meet them at the safe house and relieve Tessa so she could sleep, while a second agent would take custody of Mitch's computer and bring it over to Jerome in the IT department to be analyzed.

An unexpected contentment swept over Gabe as he reviewed their latest success with the case. Although their progress felt slow, they finally had the name of someone who seemed to be near or at the top of the organization. If they could stop Bryce Cameron, Gabe's life might actually return to some semblance of normalcy. Southern Properties no longer existed, but he could find other employment and start again in Atlanta, provided the Montalvos hadn't discovered his whereabouts. He had no idea if the Montalvos and Bryce Cameron were linked in any way, but he was sure the FBI would find a connection if one existed.

Gabe glanced over at Tessa as she drove, admiring the smoothness of her skin reflecting in the moonlight and the Christmas lights. After everything they had been through, he couldn't resist teasing her a little. "So, it seemed to bother you when I was talking to Kristy. You rolled your eyes at me."

"You know why," Tessa replied tersely. "You were flirting with her."

"I was trying to get answers. I thought that's what we needed," he said, trying to make his face look as innocent as possible.

She glanced at him once she stopped at a red light and rolled her eyes again. "Yeah, right, Mr. Smooth Talker."

He took her right hand and squeezed it gently. "I thought you liked my voice."

"I did," she said firmly, pulling her hand away. "But that was a long time ago."

Gabe laughed at her expression. "Why, Tessa McIntyre. If I didn't know better, I'd think you were jealous!"

"Jealous of what?" she scoffed. "Of you?"

"I call it like I see it, just like your friend Carl."

They came to another red light, and she turned and faced him again. He wasn't sure, but he thought he saw steam coming out of her ears. "Kristy Hartfield can have you."

"Oh really?" he said softly. Her eyes sparkled as they reflected the red and green Christmas lights from a nearby tree, and he couldn't remember her ever looking lovelier than she did right now. Suddenly, he didn't want to tease her anymore. What he wanted was Tessa back in his life. He wanted to get to know her again and see if there was any hope at reviving their relationship. Once again, the air felt electrified, and as he reached out to touch her face, she leaned slightly toward him, so that his hand cupped her cheek. Sparks of energy seemed to crackle between them as they looked into each other's eyes. "What if I want you?" he asked in a husky whisper.

FOURTEEN

A car horn honked behind them, and to Tessa's embarrassment, she realized the light had turned green and she was holding up traffic. She broke away from Gabe and his mesmerizing eyes and turned back to her driving. His question had left her completely speechless and discombobulated. She had to admit, she hadn't figured out quite yet how she felt about him. There was definitely something brewing between them, however. The air sizzled every time they were alone together. And the Christmas spirit reassured her and gave her hope. Not to mention the fact that they'd just had a major break in the case, which left her elated and reassured.

Was God granting them a second chance? It certainly seemed that way. And if God was for them, who could be against them? But now wasn't the time to analyze these thoughts. She couldn't afford to get distracted from this case or forget that someone out there was still trying to kill Gabe. Just because they'd caught a break, she did not have the luxury of slowing down to think about their future. If she let down her guard for even a moment, he could lose his life.

She changed the subject and hoped he would follow her lead. "One of the local agents told me where there are some fantastic Christmas light displays. Are you game to drive by and see them?"

Gabe leaned back, and his expression relaxed. "Sure. Looking at the lights is one of my favorite things to do during the holiday season."

"We only have a few minutes," she continued. "Other FBI agents are going to meet us at the safe house, like I said, but it's on the way."

She turned on the radio to cover the awkwardness and was rewarded with Nat King Cole singing "The Christmas Song," one that always brought back happy memories of times gone by. Gabe reached over and took her right hand again, and this time, she allowed him to hold it as she steered with her left. His warmth was reassuring and comforting, and she welcomed the support after all of the death and violence they had witnessed over the past few days.

Next came "I Heard the Bells on Christmas Day" by Casting Crowns, another one of her holiday favorites. Tessa loved the Christmas season and the focus on Jesus. She enjoyed everything about it, from the music to the giving, and especially the cooler weather and the snowy Chicago winter. It wasn't nearly as cold here in Atlanta, but the chilly air and the wonderful tunes made the atmosphere seem almost like a fairy tale and reminded her of wonderful Christmases past.

They drove in awe through the neighborhood where several of the homeowners had decorated their lawns and houses with thousands of lights. Rows of candy canes and animated deer came to life, all surrounding nativity scenes keeping the focus on the baby Jesus and His birth into the world. Each house seemed to have something new and different from the last, culminating in a white Southern-style house with large columns in the front completely draped with blue lights. The effect was stunning.

"It's just so beautiful," Tessa said softly, wondering if Gabe could hear the longing in her voice. She had wanted a family and a home she could decorate, but she had given up those dreams when Gabe had left her at the altar. Was God giving them a second chance? She just wasn't sure, and the last thing she wanted to do was make a mistake after she had gotten hurt so badly the last time. Still, she couldn't deny she had strong feelings for Gabe and that she was finally ready to let go of the past and move forward with her life. Was he going to be a part of that? A mixture of fear and hopefulness twisted in her stomach. If she fell in love with him again and then lost him once more, she wasn't sure her heart would survive it.

Gabe squeezed her hand gently and smiled, apparently not oblivious to her internal struggles. She was relieved to see patient acceptance in his eyes. "Yes, and I think this blue one is my favorite."

"Mine, too."

The street ended and Tessa turned the car out of the neighborhood and headed straight for the safe house that was only about five minutes away. There were no lights on the house, but the whole goal was to be as inconspicuous as possible, so the lack of decoration was no real surprise. They locked up the car and then headed inside. Tessa's calmness immediately disappeared, and her alertness became razor sharp as she surveyed her surroundings. She didn't know when the next threat against Gabriel would arise, but she wanted to be ready.

They entered the house, and Tessa set up the surveillance system while Gabe rummaged in the kitchen for a bite to eat. He came out with sub sandwiches a few minutes later, and Tessa hadn't realized how hungry she was until she saw the food piled high on the plate he offered her.

A few minutes later, her relief arrived, and Tessa was so exhausted that she finished her sandwich, handed off Mitch's laptop so the chain of custody was intact and headed back to her bedroom for a few hours of sleep. Gabe had been assigned the bedroom across the hall, and he had already stated he was going to bed, too, once he finished his meal. She knew the other agents that had arrived to take over the watch, and for the first time in quite a while, peace filled her heart and she slept deeply.

"So, here's what seems to be happening," Gabe said as he once again studied the flow chart he had put on giant flip-chart paper across the wall in the living room. He had gotten up at dawn and started researching money laundering schemes, so he finally felt like he had a good understanding of the case surrounding Southern Properties and Bryce Cameron. He was now ready to act as scribe as the team came together. Tessa and the other agents had joined him for breakfast, and he had fed them, as well as the new agents that had arrived at 7:00 a.m. to work the next shift, platefuls of pancakes and sausage. Now the new arrivals, along with several counterparts who were attending via a conference call app, were all gathered to discuss the latest updates and make sure everyone was on the same page. A laptop with a camera showed the faces of the various other attendees, and each of them could see Gabe as he went over the chart on the wall. Tessa had already passed along all of the updates the FBI tech team had discovered after tearing into Mitch's laptop.

"Here's how it all starts," Gabe said, pointing to a square he had drawn at the beginning of the flow chart. "Bryce Cameron receives funds from illegal activity in Europe or Africa."

"We've only been able to discover a couple of these transactions so far through the dark web and *Excelsior,* but it looks like he is selling arms to rebel factions in Africa and is also involved with human trafficking and prostitution," Tessa added.

An agent from the conference call spoke up next, and as she talked, Gabe made notes on the flow chart. "The money is then layered, or shifted, through the game with a variety of transactions designed to create confusion and complicate the trail for investigators. Some of the cash is turned into cryptocurrency and washed that way. As you know, most currencies in circulation are controlled by a centralized government, so their creation can be regulated by a third party. But since cryptocurrency's creation and transactions are open source, controlled by code and rely on peer-to-peer networks, there is no single entity or government that can affect the currency. Digital coins are stored in virtual wallets and transferred to other people's. No actual cash ever exists or changes hands."

"So are the cryptocurrencies actually purchased with dirty money?" Tessa asked.

"Yes, and then stored in a hardware wallet, which is an app on a portable device you actually plug into your laptop," the agent responded. "They can be purchased on a variety of websites and locations in the dark web, which is again what Cameron has been doing through the game *Excelsior*. The good news for Cameron is no one is tracing the cryptocurrency. The bad news is only a limited amount of dirty money can be washed that way."

Gabe moved to another page on the wall as an agent from the conference call described the next steps. "A sizable amount of the cash that Cameron needs to launder stays in cash form, so the money is deposited in small amounts and then transferred electronically into offshore bank accounts. Those offshore banks are crucial to the enterprise. Many countries, including Cyprus, have lax bank regulations that allow their customers to conceal their identities and, by extension, the source of potentially illicit funds deposited into their accounts."

Gabe made some more notes for all to see as the agent continued. Finally, everything that had been happening over the past few days was fitting together and making sense.

The agent continued. "Then, once again through the game, the account owners, either Bryce using several different accounts or associates of his representing shell companies, access the money and start investing and making purchases with it, all as part of the layering process."

Another agent from the conference call shared a document on the screen that showed a diagram of the scheme. "Here's an example. Through what we've learned from Mitch's computer, we can now tie Bryce Cameron to BRT, as well as to Glenoco and Hawks Rise Enterprises, Ltd. These two companies both have accounts in Cyprus, so they aren't required to show where they got the money that is deposited in the account. Then they bought over a million dollars' worth of antiques from a store in Williamsburg, Virginia, with a money order from the Cyprus bank. They made the purchase in January of this year and then resold the items at a profit in March. The proceeds were clean, and they could then do whatever they wanted with the money."

Tessa spoke up. "The shell corporations only existed to hold other corporate entities or assets whose ownership may or may not be anonymous. That helps conceal buyers' true identities and the sources of their funds."

"Clear as mud?" Gabe quipped.

The agents ignored Gabe's attempt at humor. "So how does your real estate firm fit into the picture?" one of the other agents asked.

Gabe shifted but was ready for the question. "Bryce Cameron must have been working with Shawn Parker. I think that's why Shawn was killed—because he knew too much about Cameron's organization. Shawn would use BRT's money to purchase real estate through our company, and Shawn must have been guiding him to properties that could easily be resold at a profit. Sometimes BRT simply invested in a property. They have massive holdings. Then they would only sell when they needed an influx of cash. They may even lose money on the sale, but that is figured in as the cost of doing business. The alternative is entirely frozen or seized accounts, and that's a worse outcome, so small losses are considered acceptable. Either way, once the property is sold a second time, the money is clean and can be used for any legitimate purpose."

A balding agent wearing a black suit was rubbing his forehead. "This stuff is giving me a headache."

"That's no surprise," Tessa said as she nodded. "I talked to the federal prosecutor earlier today to make sure we were getting her what she needed to take this case to court. She informed me that there were more than two hundred distinct federal criminal predicates for money laundering. Until she knows more, she couldn't even tell me the best way to proceed. And that's just under federal law. Several state anti–money laundering statutes complement federal statutes and hold similar penalties. If this organization is as big as we think it is, there might even be other nations waiting in line to prosecute Cameron, as well. Most countries have legal codes dealing with money laundering too, though penalties and enforcement vary greatly, and since I'm convinced we're going to take him down, we'll get the first crack at putting him behind bars."

"Is Cameron working with any USA companies to launder their money as well, or only foreign corporations?" one of the other agents asked.

"We haven't traced it all yet, so anything is possible," Tessa replied. "But our focus right now is on the international angle. What we do know is that Cameron is running BRT, and BRT has several couriers making small deposits at a bank right here in Atlanta so they can work under the radar. Deposits under 10K don't have to be reported. Then that money is also being used to buy real estate through Gabe's company and support other ventures. Once the property is bought and sold, once again, the money is clean."

"And I had no idea I was being used as a pawn in such a huge illegal operation," Gabe said, his voice filled with derision. "Shawn was handing me deals left and right, and we were making so much money on the commissions that I didn't even think to question where the money was coming from." He turned to Tessa. "Are the penalties for all of this criminal or only civil? I mean, all of this is white collar crime, right?"

Tessa shrugged. "According to the prosecutor, the United States Code offers a criminal sanction of up to twenty years in prison and a five-hundred-thousand-dollar fine, or twice the amount involved in the transaction, whichever is greater. Of course, that's the maximum, and not all cases call for the max, but I imagine this one will, even if they try plea bargaining. The civil penalties aren't as stiff, but like I said, with the size of Cameron's criminal organization, I can't imagine the prosecutor would pursue a civil remedy."

"It would be great if the US government could do something about these international banks that are involved," the balding agent said with frustration in his tone. "It sounds like the banks in Cyprus are making it easy for the Bryce Camerons of the world to prosper."

"They've tried, but it takes time," Gabe replied. "I've been doing some of my own research, and came across the case of a London-based bank that was embezzling funds for over ten years. They were making fraudulent loans and took money from more than a million depositors so they could become the personal piggy bank for its Middle Eastern owners and a few favored customers, who happened to be dictators and criminals from around the world. The bank had an 'ask no questions' policy and financed a slew of covert activities. International authorities finally shut the bank down and seized the bank's assets, but by then, the damage was already done and the remaining assets were minimal. Then the owners hid in a country that doesn't allow extradition, and they were never prosecuted."

"Good grief," Tessa said, her voice heavy. "We've got to take this guy down and make sure he pays for his crimes before he tries doing the same thing."

"So what happens next?" the balding FBI agent asked as he studied Gabe's flow chart.

Tessa stood. "I've talked this all over with Garcia. The genius behind Cameron's enterprise is that the game Mitch created keeps all of the money organized and flowing through several different areas, so Cameron always has the ability to get cash if he needs it. It's like several different roots all supporting the same tree. The cryptocurrency is one root, the real estate transactions are one root and the shell companies have other projects that represent other roots. I'm sure there are many others we haven't even discovered yet. Bryce Cameron, whoever he is, is a very powerful person."

"So, Mitch Jacobs was killed because he knew too much and had outlived his usefulness?" one of the agents asked.

"Essentially, yes. The same can be said for Shawn Parker," Tessa replied.

"Do we know how Shawn Parker was killed yet?" an agent asked from the conference call screen.

"No, the medical examiner's office is backed up. They said they'd call with the report when they get to it," Tessa stated.

"I have to say, I'm relieved there doesn't seem to be a connection to the Montalvo brothers," Gabe said. "Now, where do we go from here?" he asked as he put the cap back on the marker he had been using with a snap.

Tessa smiled, and Gabe could see she was pleased at their discoveries. The case was coming together, and Bryce Cameron would hopefully soon be within her grasp. But then what? He couldn't help wondering what was next for him. Where would he be a month from now or even next week? Would the FBI still need him? Would his life continue to be in danger? He wasn't sure what the future held, but for now, he pushed aside the questions and focused on Tessa as she explained the FBI's plans.

"One of the other roots we've discovered is shipments of cash coming to America from the Cyprus banks directly. The banks change the euros into dollars, and then the dollars are clean once they arrive on our shore. According to Mitch's game, one of these cash shipments is due to arrive tonight on a flight from Turkey. I've talked it over with Garcia, and we're going to intercept that cash. A sting is being planned as we speak."

"Do we have any idea what Bryce Cameron actually looks like?" Gabe asked.

Tessa turned. "Not a clue. There are no known photographs of him. And apparently, he has a reputation for killing anyone who gets in his way. He is a ruthless murderer. But honestly, we doubt he will be anywhere near the airport. He's probably hired a crew to intercept the cash. However, there were some other indications that Cameron is in Atlanta. We're hoping we can break his associates when we seize the cash and discover his location."

"Are you going to allow me to come to the sting at the airport?"

Tessa paused for a moment before she replied. She finally looked him in eye, and he saw worry in those green depths. "I didn't think it was such a great idea to bring you. You'll be in grave danger," Tessa answered truthfully. "But Garcia vetoed my vote. She wants you there, if you're willing to go with an FBI escort. There's an outside chance you might recognize some of the people involved since you've seen so many different players through the real estate transactions. Of course, the ability to recognize people makes you a target, too, and Cameron is probably still trying to silence you. If any of his people recognize you, you could get killed."

"Do you want me to go?" Gabe asked Tessa, trying to pin her down.

"We need you," she replied, still prevaricating. "But like I said, I think it's too dangerous. It's not my choice, though. Ultimately, it's up to you."

Gabe glanced at the other agents in the room, but none of them offered up an opinion. Still, he knew deep down what the right answer was, and ultimately, he didn't need any help making the decision. "I'm scared to go. It would be stupid of me not to be, but I feel like this is something I have to do."

Tessa looked away for a moment as if she was trying to compose herself, then turned back again to face him. "I don't want to lose you again," she said softly for his ears alone.

"Then let's do our best to make sure that doesn't happen," he replied in an equally low voice. "I trust you. I trust your team. Let's pray and make sure this plan is in line with God's will. One way or another, Bryce Cameron has to be stopped, and we might just be the way God wants to do it."

FIFTEEN

Gabe kept his eyes on the monitor, watching with fascination as the Boing 787 landed seamlessly on the tarmac and began to slow. It was the last international flight of the day coming in from the Entebbe, Uganda, and according to the manifest, it carried two hundred ninety-seven passengers plus a crew of thirteen. It also was bringing 15.8 million dollars in cash that belonged to Bryce Cameron.

Of course, the paperwork for the shipments didn't list Bryce Cameron as the owner of the cash but claimed it was the property of Glenoco, one of Cameron's shell corporations. It was also the tangible proof they needed that Glenoco was part of the money laundering scheme. While the Financial Crimes Unit was working on firming up the connections between Bryce and Glenoco by using *Excelsior* and other means, Tessa and her team were at the airport, with search warrants and court orders in hand, ready to seize the cash.

Gabe glanced in Tessa's direction. Instead of her normal everyday suit, she was now clad in her battle dress uniform—black pants and a long-sleeved shirt, with her hair pulled back in a ponytail. She was also wearing a bullet-proof vest that had FBI emblazoned on the front and back. She was every inch the professional, and Gabe had no doubts she would make a truly inspirational Special Agent in Charge once she was promoted. He was excited about the opportunity the promotion offered her. The SAC job involved overseeing all of the Chicago operations and carried a large amount of responsibility. In his eyes, she was a perfect fit. But would she want him when she finally had her dream job? Would there be room in her life for both?

Gabe and Tessa had ensconced themselves in one of the security rooms on the second floor of the airport and had the room to themselves once the security officer had shown them the ropes with the equipment and then moved on to his other duties. The rest of Tessa's team was out on the tarmac, working with others from the airport security team who would help secure the cash once the seizure was effectuated.

Movement on another camera caught Gabe's eye, and he turned his focus back to the new video feed that showed an unmarked truck at the cargo gate where semis routinely entered the airport's property to retrieve their shipments. A driver showed his identification badge and then signed a form at the security checkpoint. A moment later, he handed the clipboard and pen back to the officer manning the gate.

"Do you recognize the driver?" Tessa asked as she looked back and forth between the monitor and Gabe's expression.

"No, he's a stranger to me. Can we get a better view of his partner in the passenger seat?"

Tessa made the request through a headset, and as Gabe watched, the camera moved slightly and focused more on the passenger. Gabe leaned closer so he could get an even better view. The passenger had shortly cropped dark hair and was sporting a goatee, but even though the man's high cheekbones and European appearance looked familiar at first, upon taking a second look, Gabe realized he didn't know the man after all.

A knock on the door interrupted them and Tessa went to answer it while Gabe stayed seated, his eyes glued to the monitor. There was a disturbance at the back of the room by the door, and the next thing he knew, Tessa was out cold on the floor and a tall, muscular man with dark brown hair was stepping over her and pointing a gun with a silencer straight at Gabe's chest. He was wearing the red coat and blue tie of one of the airlines, complete with a security badge, but it was clear he was no airline employee. A shorter man wearing a janitor's uniform entered next. He grabbed Tessa's arms and dragged her motionless body into the room, then closed the door tightly behind him. Once they were all inside, he dropped her carelessly back on the floor in a heap. He searched her roughly and took her phone and headset, then put both on the ground and stomped on them, breaking the headset into small pieces and grinding the phone under his boot.

Gabe slowly raised his hands as adrenaline and fear coursed within him. He started to protest at their rough treatment of Tessa but then thought better of it. If they knew she mattered to him, they might use it against him and hurt her just to spite him. Hopefully, if they thought he was indifferent to her fate, they would leave her alone. He could tell by their expressions and body language that they were all business and would do whatever was necessary to achieve their objective. At this point, he needed every advantage he had if he wanted to keep them both alive. Still, it hurt his heart to see her unconscious body lying prone on the floor, and he knew she was going to have a fierce headache when she awoke.

"Get up," the first man said as he motioned with his weapon. The man had a strong accent Gabe couldn't quite place, and there was an emptiness in his eyes that made Gabe even more on edge. He complied with the man's orders, keeping his hands visible and his motions slow and nonthreatening.

"No sudden movements," the man ordered, despite Gabe's obvious cooperation. "Put your arms out." The second man pulled out his gun and held it on Gabe while the first stowed his weapon and frisked Gabe from head to toe. Finding no weapon, he pulled out his gun again and kept it trained on Gabe's chest. "Keep your hands up where I can see them at all times, understand? Now go out the door." The dark-haired man gave him a push, and his tone left no room for argument.

Gabe complied, and the two men followed him out into the hallway. He stopped when he came to another door that had a keypad, and the man masquerading as the janitor approached and punched in the key, then pushed Gabe through it. They ended up on a small metal landing facing the tarmac outside the building. Dusk was upon them, and the fading light in the horizon was supplemented by the large lights that illuminated the flight line, the planes and the workers like a football field. A wind of cold, humid air hit them as they went outside, but Gabe barely felt it due to the adrenaline flowing through him. Where were they taking him? Were they going to finish what the other gunmen that had shot at him failed to do? He glanced around the airport, wondering if his last sight on earth was going to be the concrete tarmac below his feet.

A sense of dread assaulted him and for a moment he felt frozen, watching the movement and area around him but unable to even form another coherent thought. Loading beds with trailers zoomed around the jets, carrying luggage between the aircraft and the airport, and cargo box vehicles loaded meals and drinks alongside other planes that were readying to take off and fly to parts unknown. He shivered involuntarily, which broke his trance. Were these the last things he was ever going to see? Regret pierced him so strongly that he suddenly felt an actual physical pain his chest. Why hadn't he told Tessa how he felt about her?

He didn't want to die like this. He forced himself to remain calm and focus on his situation. There had to be a way out. He said a silent prayer, asking God to show him how and when to escape this horrible situation.

The man wearing the janitor's uniform pushed Gabe from behind and motioned for him to move toward the steps leading to the tarmac. "Head down the stairs. Now."

Gabe took a step, then turned suddenly and slammed his fist into the dark-haired man's stomach. His second blow caught the shorter man in the jaw, and then he kicked out and caught the first man in the hand with his left foot, causing his gun to go flying. The janitor impersonator was quick to recover, but before he could act, Gabe had a strong hold on his weapon and had wrenched it from his hand. He turned the weapon toward the two mercenaries and held it steady, moving it only slightly as he aimed back and forth between the two targets. Both of the men froze when they realized Gabe had both the weapon and the advantage, and they put their hands up in surrender.

"Turn and put your hands on the door, both of you!" Gabe ordered.

They did as he asked, and although Gabe was wary and distrustful, he approached them and quickly frisked them with his free hand, making sure they had no other weapons to surprise him. Gabe didn't find any guns or knives, but he did find several zip ties in the dark-haired man's jacket and he pulled them out, as well as both of their phones. He pocketed the phones, then motioned toward the metal handrail.

"Okay, zip-tie your friend to the railing," he commanded, keeping the gun trained on the man's midriff.

"You won't get away with this," the taller man muttered under his breath as he took the zip ties. "You'll be lucky if you're still alive by midnight."

"Maybe you should worry about your own future," Gabe returned caustically. "In a few short hours, you'll be heading to prison."

The dark-haired man gave him a disbelieving smirk but tied his accomplice's hands to the railing as he was told, then zip-tied his own feet together with the largest of the ties when Gabe ordered him to do so. Gabe wasn't sure that would help much, but he hoped it would at least keep the man from attacking him while he made sure the man tightly confined his own hands. These two were obviously hired muscle, and since Gabe was neither trained nor experienced in police tactics or self-defense, he was operating with an abundance of caution sprinkled with a small amount of creativity.

Once he felt like they were secure, or at least as secure as he could make them, he tried the door that led back into the building, just in case. Unfortunately, it had locked behind them, and a key code was required to get back in. Gabe pointed his gun at the shorter man.

"Punch in the key," he ordered.

The man glared at him. "No."

No? Gabe was surprised by the man's answer. On TV, the bad guys always complied when they had a gun pointed at him. What was he doing wrong? Gabe reached out and grabbed the taller man's ID badge from his jacket and tried it on the slot on the security lock by the door. The red light remained constant—the door was still locked. Apparently, the man's fake badge wouldn't open the door. "You put in the code," Gabe ordered the taller man.

"No," the man replied, his eyes boring into him. "I don't think you'll actually shoot me."

A cold sweat swept down Gabe's spine. The offender was right. Gabe didn't have it in him to shoot an unarmed man, not even to get back inside the building and continue the mission. But now what? How else could he force these mercenaries to do what he needed?

Tessa groaned as she regained consciousness. The attacker had hit her chin with the heel of his hand the second she had opened the door, and she hadn't even gotten a good look at the man. The movement had instantly snapped her head back and pinched the nerves at the top of the spinal column, knocking her out. Now she had a headache and a sore chin, but thankfully, she was otherwise unharmed. She sat up a little too quickly but took a moment to recover and then stood, studying her surroundings.

Gabe was nowhere to be found.

A wave of fear swept over her. They had obviously taken him—but where? If they were going to kill him anyway, why not just do it here? Her thoughts swirled in her mind as she considered her next move. She reached for her phone but then noticed it was in a broken heap on the floor. She picked it up anyway and tried to power it on, but it wouldn't start. She stuck it in the side pocket of her pants, hoping that at some point she could at least retrieve the information on the SIM card, and then reached for the landline phone on the desk. All she heard through the handset was a hissing sound and no dial tone. She imagined that Cameron's team had disabled the lines, but regardless, she currently had no way to contact her team from this room or alert them to what was happening. If Cameron's men had found Gabe, then they must know about the seizure that was about to go down. She had to get to that plane as soon as possible and warn her comrades before anyone else was hurt. She said a prayer, asking for God's help, and quickly left the room, heading for the tarmac.

SIXTEEN

Gabe stowed the gun in his waistband and took the stairs to the tarmac, leaving the two men strapped to the handrail. There was no one around at this part of the airport, and he didn't see any doors available that didn't also have the telltale security pad that kept him from reentering the building. His only choice was to head to where the flight from Uganda had landed and try to warn the FBI agents that Tessa had been hurt and the sting had been compromised. The Atlanta Hartsfield-Jackson International Airport was huge, and one of the busiest in the world. The only positive note was that they were currently at the international terminal, which was separated from the main domestic terminal by a twelve-minute shuttlebus ride. Thankfully, the international terminal was much smaller than the domestic version, and only had twelve gates on concourse F, where they had been waiting for the flight to arrive. Even so, the security room video feed was on the opposite side of the airport terminal from where he needed to be, and he looked frantically around him for a way to speed up his trip. A small tug vehicle was abandoned nearby and still had the key in the ignition. It wasn't one of the bigger ones that was used for pushing the larger international planes, and Gabe imagined it was being used by someone who just needed to get around the runway without getting in the way or maybe to pull the luggage racks he'd seen when the baggage men unloaded and loaded the planes. The tug had a windshield but otherwise looked like a souped-up tractor, and Gabe realized he'd be lucky if the vehicle drove much faster than he could run. Still, he had a long way to go, and the tug was better than nothing. He brought the engine to life with a roar and started turning the vehicle to the left so he could leave the area.

"Hey! Where are you going? Get out of that vehicle!" A man wearing a jumpsuit who obviously worked at the airport started yelling at him and running in his direction. He was about thirty feet away but was closing in fast. Gabe ignored the man and slammed his foot onto the gas pedal. As he'd thought, the airport tug wasn't designed for speed, especially when turning. In fact, the man was able to get close enough to grab Gabe's shirt and give it a hard pull before he had gone very far at all, but Gabe yanked himself free, keeping his foot on the gas and his hands on the steering wheel. The tug slowly pulled away from the man, who was still yelling at him as he tried to climb on board the tug or pull Gabriel off. Gabe leaned forward, thankful when the tug finally escaped his pursuer. He turned to gauge the man's position and noticed the worker had stopped running but was now raising his fist in anger with one hand and using his phone with the other, presumably to call in the theft. He looked a second time and saw the man rubbing his shoulder and pacing back and forth, obviously angry.

Since Gabe needed to find the FBI anyway, he wasn't too worried about the man's call and thought it might actually be a blessing instead of a problem in the long run. The man might not have believed his story if he'd just tried to explain what was happening, and this way, security would get a call regardless and would hopefully put the dots together and understand that the sting had been compromised. He turned and faced straight again, going as fast as the vehicle could carry him to the site where the Ugandan flight had stopped and unloaded its passengers.

He could see the plane in the distance and smiled as relief swept over him. He was close. Really close. There were a lot of people working around the various planes, and a few workers looked up as he drove by, but just as many others ignored him since they were busy doing their own jobs. He slowed and then stopped as an Airbus A320 pushed back from the terminal, and he waited impatiently so he could get around the plane without causing a problem for the pilot or the passengers.

The first shot hit the dashboard of the small tug, only inches away from his hand on the steering wheel. He turned, frantically searching for the shooter, and saw a rifle sticking out of a window of a tanker as it approached him rather quickly from behind. He still had the gun he'd taken from the man in the janitor's uniform, but he was hesitant to fire back at the shooter since the truck was probably filled with gasoline and might hurt not only the men chasing him but also innocent by-standers if it exploded.

The second shot whizzed by his ear and shattered the windshield, and a third did the same, inches from where the other bullet hit. Bits of glass flew at his face as he continued driving, head down and scrunched in the seat the best he could, toward the Ugandan flight. The sound of gunfire caused quite a commotion on the tarmac, and workers ducked and ran to get away from it.

Gabe zigzagged the vehicle and continued to crouch as low as possible in the seat, hoping he was making for a very small and difficult-to-hit target. He heard sirens behind him but kept moving as more bullets rained down upon him. One shot finally took out his left front tire, and the tug swerved and became impossible to handle. He pulled hard against the steering wheel, and the truck came to a screeching halt as he slammed down on the brake pedal. He glanced over his shoulder and saw that the tanker truck was only a few yards behind him, bearing down fast. He jumped from the vehicle just in time as the tanker slammed into the tug with a loud crash, and he heard the horrible squeal of metal scraping against metal. Smoke and gasoline spewed around the wreckage, and then suddenly, the tanker erupted into flames with a large explosion that shot fire high up into the air, lighting up the night sky.

Tessa had been running through the terminal to reach the gate where the passengers had already disembarked from the Ugandan flight when she heard the crash and explosion from inside the terminal. The blast could be felt inside the building, and several onlookers rushed to the windows at the sound of the explosion and watched as the flames licked the sky. Her heart was beating in overdrive as she skidded to a stop and flashed her badge to the airport security personnel guarding the Jetway. They let her pass, but she ordered them to keep everyone else out as she hurried down the long hallway, and she took one of the officers with her. Silently, she said a fervent prayer for the safety of her FBI team as she reached the area where the Jetway was pushed against the door of the plane, but instead of going on the plane, she pointed toward the door leading down the stairs that that baggage handlers used to bring up unusually sized baggage or other special items.

"Open that, Officer Kelley," she commanded

as she added his name after examining his nameplate. She pulled her weapon, not sure what she was going to find on the other side of the door. "Get ready. We have a situation here, and have FBI and a civilian witness on the scene. The agents are wearing vests identifying themselves, but I imagine there are some others here trying to steal a large pallet of cash from the plane."

"This plane isn't going anywhere," the officer confirmed. "I checked with the airline when they sent us over. It's due to spend the night here at the gate and leave at zero-six-thirty tomorrow for a flight back to Entebbe."

"Good to know," she agreed. That confirmed what they had discovered when they first set up this operation. "We have a court order to seize the shipment of cash, Officer, and I'm going to need your help. There are some who don't want that to happen, so keep your eyes open and be ready for anything."

The officer nodded as she turned and took the steps two at a time down the metal staircase. The officer followed her to the tarmac, his pistol also pulled and ready.

Mass confusion met her at the bottom of the stairs, as well as a wave of heat from fire that permeated the humid, sticky night air, even though it was at least a hundred yards away. The smell of burning gasoline, rubber and plastic was overpowering, and she put her arm up and blocked what she could with her shirtsleeve as she advanced. Black smoke swirled around the two vehicles that had crashed, and the plane had been abandoned by the uniformed workers who had rushed to the site of the accident and appeared to be searching for survivors.

A fire engine was approaching, as well as several other vehicles, and she saw a mass of yellow and red lights heading in their direction. Tessa kept her weapon ready and slowly circled the wheel well at the front of the plane but saw no sign of her FBI counterparts. In fact, no one was where she expected them to be—no baggage handlers or other airport staff were anywhere around the plane. She kept to the shadows, wanting to figure out what was happening before she made her presence known to anyone that might show up at the scene. A bitter wind blew against her cheek as the cold night air chilled her. Where were the FBI? Where was Gabe?

An empty baggage car attached to a tug engine was abandoned nearby, and Tessa slowly approached it, her gun pointing to the sky.

When she reached it, she turned quickly and aimed her gun into the first compartment. Three suitcases were inside, as well as the bodies of two FBI agents. She quickly felt for pulses on both men and was able to find them without too much difficulty. A third body was in the second compartment. All of the men were still alive and breathing, but they had been knocked out, zip-tied and gagged. She tried unsuccessfully to rouse them, making her believe they had probably been drugged before they were secured.

"Keep your eyes open," she commanded Officer Kelley.

Suddenly she heard a nearby sound as a hydraulic lift operated, and she saw a wooden crate on a pallet being slowly raised by a forklift and placed on the back of a food truck that had just arrived on the scene. It appeared to be an ordinary delivery from a local food company to restock the plane, but Tessa knew differently. For one thing, the pallet was being loaded onto the food truck, not being unloaded, as one would expect. Second, it wasn't food being transported, but rather a large bundle of cash the size of a small storage shed, encased in plastic wrap.

She heard a bullet whiz by her and turned

just in time to see Officer Kelley's eyes round and a look of surprise cover his features. Then slowly, she could just make out a stain of red as it bloomed around the small hole in his chest. He glanced down at his torso and then slowly fell forward, first to his knees, and then his entire body slumped on the concrete. Tessa knew he was dead before he even hit the ground. She darted behind the truck and crouched close to the ground, seeking refuge from the violent onslaught. Six more bullets flew in her direction before she dared to peek around the wheels of the trailer. She could see two pairs of boots coming in her direction, and once they got about thirty feet away, they split up so they could go around both ends of the vehicle and cut off her escape.

She counted to ten in her head to calm her nerves, then rolled under the trailer. When she came out the other side, she immediately pointed her weapon and emerged shooting.

SEVENTEEN

Gabe's body rolled from the force of the jump, and when he finally stopped, he felt like an elephant was sitting on his chest because it was so hard to breathe. He lay still for a moment, inventorying his injuries, and decided that while he was scraped up, nothing was seriously wrong with any part of him. As his breath slowly returned, he pulled himself up to a sitting position, then finally made it to his feet.

"Are you okay?" a man asked, mere seconds before a bullet hit the newcomer in the chest and he fell at Gabe's feet. Gabe instantly raised his hands as the shooter approached, his eyes never leaving the barrel of the .45 revolver that was pointed at his chest. He felt the gun he had taken from the mercenary in his waistband, but he didn't want to take a chance drawing it on the criminal heading straight for him. He wasn't trained in firearms, and his actions would undoubtedly cause the man to fire without really giving himself a good chance of survival.

The gunman approached Gabe carefully, then frisked him and confiscated the weapon and secured it in his own pocket. Then he circled Gabe and pushed him from behind. "Head toward that truck, now," he said in a menacing voice as he motioned at a food truck next to the plane.

"Okay, no problem," Gabe answered, trying to keep his voice level and calm. The last thing he wanted to do was give this man a reason to shoot him. Although he doubted he would survive this encounter anyway, a seed of hope grew within him that somehow, some way, Tessa, or the other FBI agents on the scene, would discover his predicament and intervene.

The man forced him to go to the back of the vehicle, which was still open. Two others had just finished loading a pallet into the truck bed, and he glanced carefully at the new faces. He didn't recognize either one of them for sure, but the one holding the gun on him looked vaguely familiar. He wondered fleetingly if the man was one of the couriers he had seen making deposits at the bank but couldn't immediately place him. His current predicament made it hard for him to even think straight. Maybe the man who had said he would be dead by midnight had had a point.

"Inside," the shooter ordered, waving his gun toward the back of the truck.

"Where are we going?" Gabe asked, his hands still up in a motion of surrender. He was surprised he didn't see any FBI agents anywhere around, and the hope he had been feeling turned to dread when he realized the cavalry probably wasn't going to show up and save his hide after all.

"To see an old friend," the shooter replied.

"Old friend?" Gabe repeated, still playing for time. He didn't know what had happened to the FBI agents, but he hoped that if could delay the inevitable, even for a few moments, it just might give them time to arrive on the scene. The plane was abandoned as the workers who would normally be swarming around were still attending to the crash site and trying to extinguish the flames. A fire engine had arrived on the scene, and several airport security cars were flitting around the crash site and ignoring the activity by the airplane and the cargo transfer. If Gabe had planned it himself, he couldn't have created a more perfect diversion. But where were these armed men going to take him? He was in no hurry to die, but he couldn't help wondering why they just didn't shoot him outright. With noise from the fire engine and emergency vehicles, he doubted one more gunshot would really cause a problem. Who wanted to meet him, and why?

"No more questions," the man ordered as he broke through Gabriel's train of thought. He approached Gabe again and pushed him toward the back of the truck. "Get in, now."

The bullet came from his left, and slowly, the man who had been pointing the gun at him sank to the ground. Gabe didn't wait to find out why. He crouched low to the ground, then rolled under the truck that had the pallet inside. Unfortunately, he was unarmed now, but he had a good view of the shooter from behind the tire, and he watched in fascination as the scene played out in front of him.

Tessa steadied herself against the side of the wheel well by the front of the plane and took careful aim. She fired again, this time taking out the criminal who was running by the side of the truck and holding a rifle. He fell hard, and at the same time, Gabe heard the engine roll over from the truck above him. He moved so the truck tire wouldn't hit him as it pulled away but stayed on the ground, hoping to keep out of the line of fire. She fired again, hitting the passenger-side door of the truck as it pulled away. Once the truck had moved about twenty feet and Gabe was clear, she steadied her aim once more and shot out the rear two tires of the vehicle, one by one. The truck continued for a few hundred feet as sparks flew from the metal as the rubber gave way and the wheels grinded against the cement. Then the truck slowly came to a stop.

Tessa glanced over at Gabe, and, seeing that he seemed okay, she ran to the side of the truck, her gun trained on the driver's-side door. She approached from the side of the vehicle, her voice firm. "FBI! Put both hands out the window, now!"

A moment passed, then another. Finally, the driver put two hands out the window. Even though the light was dim, she could see that a wound on his left hand had blood trickling down the man's arm. Hopefully, since he was injured, he would surrender without hurting anyone else.

She hadn't seen a passenger on the other side of the truck, but in an abundance of caution, she didn't just assume the driver was by himself. Several of the nearby officers that had been attending to the crash came up behind her, lending her support as they realized what was happening and recognized that she was a lone FBI agent trying to effectuate the arrest.

"We've got your back, agent!" one of them with sergeant stripes on his sleeve yelled.

Tessa acknowledged the help and continued advancing on the truck. When she got close enough to the door, she opened it, then quickly pointed her weapon at the driver. He kept his hands visible, and she could see that he had a wound on his left hand and on his right shoulder.

"Out of the truck. Now!" she ordered.

The man complied, even though she could tell he was struggling to use his right hand due to his injury.

"On your knees!" she commanded once he was free of the vehicle. She hurriedly glanced inside, verifying that he was the only occupant of the truck. Once she felt safe, she approached from behind while the sergeant from the airport security force came up in front of the man and kept his weapon pointed at the offender's midriff. She pulled his hands behind him and cuffed him, trying not to be too rough since the man was injured, but tempering that concern with the knowledge that the man was a dangerous killer and would have shot her with no remorse if he'd been able to do so. Once he was secured, she pulled him to his feet and handed him off to the sergeant, who took him by the arm and led him toward the terminal.

She turned then and looked for Gabe, who was standing next to another officer. He too had been handcuffed, but she had missed the event since she was so involved in stopping the truck.

She approached the two and met Gabe's eyes that were filled with concern.

"Are you okay?" they both asked each other at the same time.

Tessa smiled. "Yeah, I'll survive. You look a little worse for wear." He was covered with scrapes and road burn from his jump from the truck. She turned to the security guard who had cuffed him. "Officer, this man is with the FBI and is part of our team that was sent here to effectuate a court order. I suggest you remove those handcuffs right now."

"But, ma'am, he stole a vehicle…"

"A fact we will sort out with your supervisor during the debriefing," she stated in her firmest FBI voice. "For now, release him. I'll take full responsibility for any resulting repercussions." She motioned toward the baggage carts. "And call an ambulance immediately and direct them to that cart over there. Three of our agents are down and need medical assistance ASAP. I think they've been drugged."

The young officer nodded. "Yes, ma'am." He removed the handcuffs and made the call and headed over to the trailer where she had found her team earlier.

Gabe rubbed his wrists and smiled. "That feels much better." He glanced over at the wreck where the fire department had doused the flames and the charred remains lay steaming from the mixture of foam and other chemicals that had been sprayed on the fire to put it out. Then he looked at the truck with the damaged tires that held the money. "Looks like Bryce Cameron is in for a surprise. I'll bet he'll be a little unhappy when he learns he's missing 15.8 million dollars from his coffers."

"And yet, I'm having trouble feeling sorry for him," Tessa quipped. "Can you hang out for a while? It's going to take some time to get this scene under control and make sure we take custody of that cash."

"Sure." He reached into his pocket and handed her the cell phones he had taken off the two assailants earlier when he had tied them to the handrails. They both had cracked screens from his jump from the truck but were otherwise undamaged. "I took these phones from the guys that knocked you out back in the security room. If they're still there and haven't been discovered by some of their cohorts, they're zip-tied to the railing on the metal landing near where we were working. You might want to send someone over to collect them."

Tessa raised an eyebrow. "Impressive, Mr. Real Estate. Looks like hanging around the FBI is starting to wear off on you. Pretty soon, you'll be wanting to make arrests on your own."

"Not hardly," Gabe said as he winced and adjusted his shoulder. "Once this is over, I'll be happy as can be to go back to the quiet life. If such a thing is possible, that is." He glanced around the busy tarmac. "Any place in particular I should wait?"

Tessa looked for the safest, most well-lit location where she could keep an eye on him while also working the scene. "If you don't mind, stay outside and over there by the doorway," she said, motioning with her hand.

Gabe took a step forward and met Tessa's eyes. When he spoke, his words were soft so only she could hear them. "You scared me tonight. I thought I'd lost you."

She didn't pull away from his gaze, and instead, met his look head-on. Something told her that he wasn't just talking about when she had gotten knocked out back at the security surveillance room.

Gabe continued, his voice still soft. "I love you, Tessa. Let's try again. Please." He raised his hand and gently cupped her face, then softly ran his thumb along her cheek. Fire seemed to fly from his fingertips and her skin tingled at his touch. "I won't push." He continued in that radio voice when she didn't answer him. "But think about it, okay?" His thumb moved to her lips and lightly traced their contours.

"I can't…think about this right now," she finally replied, suddenly breaking free of the web he had spun around her. With extreme effort, she tore her eyes away, took a deep breath and then stopped a tall, lanky officer who was walking by. She flashed her badge and then pointed toward Gabe. The man was suitably impressed by her FBI credentials and stood erect before her. "Officer, I'm Tessa McIntyre with the FBI. I need you to guard this man and keep him safe until further notice. Is that understood? He's a federal witness and vital to the case."

"Yes, ma'am," the man responded with a clipped, respectful tone. Gabe and the officer headed over to the area where she had suggested, and she turned and hurried over to the FBI agents that had been drugged to verify they were still alive and check on their condition. Two EMTs who had been called for the initial crash were already on the scene and evaluating the men, and another ambulance was approaching, sirens blazing.

After all three men were loaded up into the ambulances, Tessa was finally convinced the agents were in good hands. She turned back to verify Gabe was safe and being guarded by the officer.

Neither man was visible. Gabriel Grayson and the officer had disappeared.

EIGHTEEN

"How did they even realize we had a sting planned for the airport?" one of the agents asked the group of other FBI agents gathered around the conference table. They were about to watch the video feed from the airport, and there was tension in the air due to the many failures that had occurred during the operation.

Garcia turned and faced the agent. "Unfortunately, they bribed the judicial assistant to warn them if a warrant was ever signed that would jeopardize the cash deliveries. The woman was drowning in medical bills for her spouse who has cancer, so she was particularly vulnerable."

"Here's what we think happened," the SAC, Sonja Garcia, said as she started the feed. "This man, dressed as airport security, took Gabriel Grayson to the terminal." They watched as the two men walked to where Tessa had ordered them to go, then looked closely at the feed where they could just make out the shape of a handgun in the officer's hand, pointing at Gabe. "The imposter then walked him into the building and out to a waiting van with stolen plates."

The SAC turned back toward the screen at the front of the room and pushed a button on her remote. The monitor instantly changed to a shot of the face of Gabe's abductor. Next to it, a new photo popped up from a foreign passport. The man was blond with brown eyes and a mole on his left cheek. "Facial recognition software identified the man as Martin Andreiko, a gun for hire from Ukraine."

"Any idea why they took him instead of just killing him outright?" one of the agents asked.

"None," Garcia responded. "After taking shots at him several times over the past few days, we can't explain why they abducted him instead, but regardless, we want to recover him before they decide to change their minds."

Tessa approached and handed Garcia a document. "We've found a connection, thanks to the phones Gabe retrieved from those two men who tried to abduct him that he zip-tied to the handrail."

"Pull up their pictures," Garcia ordered, and two more passport-type photos appeared on the screen in front of the group of agents.

"Their names are Ivan Sirko and Danilo Pavlychko. Again, both known as Ukrainian mercenaries for hire, and both with previous arrest records for petty crimes in Ukraine."

"So, what's the connection to Cameron?" Garcia asked, her tone hopeful.

"We found some texts on Sirko's phone between him and a Caz, which we think is a code name for Cameron. They discuss a meet that is scheduled for tonight at 7:00 p.m. at a warehouse near the local zoo," Tessa replied.

"Don't you think they've rescheduled, now that they've got Gabe and we've got the money?"

"What I think is that they're going to ask to exchange the money for Gabe. But whether they do or not, I believe the location is still important, because I think that's where they're holding Gabe. Even if Cameron isn't there, we need to check it out."

"What if you're wrong?" Garcia asked.

"Then we go through with the exchange and put every tracer we can think of on the money." She took a step forward. "But I think I'm right, and I think we have a chance to save Gabriel Grayson right now by sending in a strike team."

At that moment, Tessa's new cell phone rang, and the number calling showed up as "unidentified." The office quieted, just in case the call was from the abductors, and as the voice began speaking, they weren't disappointed.

"I have your man." The voice was mechanically distorted, and Tessa looked at their phone specialist, who shook her head, noting that they were struggling to trace the call while she talked, and so far, hadn't been successful. That also meant she needed to drag the call out as long as possible to give them the time they needed to run a proper trace.

"And?" Tessa asked.

"I want my money back," the voice demanded.

"Take it to the courts," Tessa said, not wanting to seem too eager to please. "Our seizure was legal, and we have a court order to prove it."

"Legal or not, you're going to give it back to me, or I'm going to kill Gabriel Grayson."

"How do I know you're not going to just

kill him anyway?" Tessa asked, steeling her voice and responding to the agent who was motioning for her to make the call continue.

"I guess you'll just have to trust me," the mechanical voice stated.

Tessa paused, hoping her delay would make the caller think she was considering his offer. Finally, she responded. "I can't just stick 15.8 million dollars in my pocket. That's a large amount of cash. And I can't just leave it on a park bench somewhere, either."

"Put the money in the back of an unmarked truck, and park the truck in the Atlanta Zoo parking lot in section A-4. Leave the keys in the ignition. Once I verify the money has been returned and there are no tracers included, I'll release your man."

"I need proof of life," Tessa demanded. "Right here, right now. If you can't produce Grayson..."

There was a clicking sound, and then suddenly there was a new voice on the phone. "Hello, Agent McIntyre? This is Gabe. I'm okay."

Tessa's hand involuntarily tightened. "Hold on, Mr. Grayson. We're doing everything we can to secure your release."

"I trust you," Gabe told her.

Seconds later, the mechanical voice returned. "Park the truck in the designated area by 7:00 p.m. tonight. No tracers. No cops. Got it? If I see anyone but you driving the truck, I'll kill him. You can walk to the MARTA bus stop after you drop it off. Don't forget, I'll be watching you the entire way. If anything or anyone stops me from getting my money back, I'll kill him."

"I understand," Tessa responded, her voice strained. She glanced over at the phone specialist, whose face made a frustrating expression the second the mechanical voice hung up. "That call was bouncing around so many locations, I had no way of tracking it down in that small amount of time. I'm sorry. I did my best."

"Not your fault," Tessa said quietly. She turned back to Garcia. "Well?"

"Assemble your strike team," Garcia stated firmly. "Let's raid that warehouse and see if we can get Mr. Grayson released safely."

Tessa nodded grimly, remembering Gabe's words before he had left the tarmac. *I love you. Let's try again.* Oh, how the idea tempted her. But what bothered her the most was that she had been a coward. She, Tessa McIntyre, soon to be the new SAC in the Chicago office, had been too scared to tell Gabe how she was really feeling, and now she might never get the chance to tell him that she loved him. And she did, she realized, even if she had discovered it belatedly. She couldn't deny the feelings that had been revived and were now growing inside her once again. She loved Gabriel Grayson, and this love was a new, more mature sentiment than anything she remembered feeling in the past. What would she do if she never got the chance to tell him?

She resolved two things at that very moment. The first was that from now on, she was going to tell the ones she cared about how she felt so there was never any ambiguity. The second was that tonight, they were going to rescue Gabriel and solve this case, or she was going to die trying.

Gabe looked up through swollen eyes, the result of his failed escape attempt. He'd gotten several bruises from his efforts, as well as a cut lip and a cracked rib, if he was reading the pain in his side correctly. Now he was sitting in a wooden chair, his hands and feet tied to it, and he had a very limited range of motion. He was waiting. For whom or what, he wasn't sure. But the three men who had brought him here a couple of hours ago had made it clear they were on standby until someone important arrived.

He licked his cracked lips and tasted the metallic flavor of blood. They had really beaten him quite severely when he'd tried to escape. Now he was hurting, thirsty and even a bit hungry, but all of those considerations were overridden by the fierce need for survival that was gripping his heart. He didn't want to die today, but that possibility was appearing more and more likely with each passing minute. He had no illusions about his fate. Even though Gabe had been told that the FBI was going to trade his life for the money that had been seized in the airport raid, he had seen too many faces, and he doubted their sincerity.

"Mr. Cameron has arrived, and he's heading this way."

Gabe heard the men guarding the door whispering, and anxiety forced beads of sweat to form on his brow, despite the chilly temperature in the room. Now he knew he was slated for death with absolute certainty. If he was scheduled to see the head of this organization face-to-face, there was no way they would let him live.

At least Gabe was going to finally meet the man who had thrown his life into complete and utter chaos before his life was taken, but it was a small and disappointing consolation prize in this giant game of theft and deceit.

He thought back over the past few days and found solace in the fact that Tessa had forgiven him. Even though she hadn't pronounced her feelings, he knew the relationship had been healed significantly. He'd hoped for more but thanked God that he'd at least had a chance to make amends for leaving her without an explanation and had been able to apologize for the pain he had caused. That reconciliation had given him a peace that had eluded him for the past three years.

He pulled helplessly against his bindings as anger and fear swirled together and made his chest feel tight. There was so much more he wanted to do with his life, and now, he would never get that chance.

Swishing fabric and falling footsteps sounded near the door, but Gabe had no way to turn and look as he heard several men enter the room. A large, burly black man grabbed a chair and placed it about four feet in front of Gabe and then stepped back as another man, dressed in a very expensive suit and shoes, appeared and took off his topcoat. The newcomer turned and handed his coat to another large man in a black suit and tie who was standing to his left, and Gabe strained to see his face but wasn't successful. If he was going to be killed today, he at least wanted to see the face of his executioner before he died. He strained to move to the left so he could get a better view, but all Gabe could see was the newcomer's back as he talked softly to one of his men. Then suddenly, Bryce Cameron turned and took off his dark glasses at the same time that he gave Gabe a winning smile.

Gabe's eyes widened and surprise hit him like a literal belt to the gut.

Shawn Parker stood before him, and he most certainly wasn't dead.

"Hello, Gabe," Shawn said, his voice smooth. He straightened his tie, then leaned forward and gave Gabe a direct look. "You've looked better, my friend."

Gabe was incredulous. How could this man be alive? He'd seen the burned body, the watch, the clothes. Even knowing that it must have been an elaborate ruse based on the truth of seeing the man standing before him, it was hard to accept. "So your real name is Bryce

Cameron." He shook his head, still trying to wrap his head around the concept. "I thought we were friends. I must have been mistaken."

"We were friends," Shawn continued. "We made a lot of money together. I was even ready to bring you on board as a person of power within my organization, but then I discovered your past, Ethan."

A cold chill ran down Gabe's spine as Shawn used his real name. Only someone who knew his past and that he had been in witness protection would know that information.

"I can see from your expression that I've shocked you. But let me tell you, anyone with the kind of money I have acquired and the proper motivation can find out anything they need to know about anyone on the planet. And I needed to know everything I could discover about you before I welcomed you into my organization in any capacity. But once I knew that you had given up everything in your old life and testified against the Montalvos, I realized I could never trust you. You would always want to play the white knight, always stand on your principles, even when there was a heap of money to be made."

"There's nothing wrong with being honest and treating people fairly," Gabe declared firmly. "Life isn't all about money."

Shawn laughed, a deep, throaty sound that Gabe remembered so well. "Do you realize how naive you sound?" He shook his head as if lecturing a recalcitrant child. "I'm the leader of an immense international syndicate. I can buy and sell anything to anyone. Perhaps you should stop lecturing me for a minute and really think about what you're missing. Don't you understand the amount of power I have?"

"Sure," Gabe responded, his voice level. "But money can't buy love. It can't buy happiness. And no amount of power can create a relationship with Jesus. Sunsets are free, my friend, but they offer a fleeting beauty no one can purchase. You're the one missing out on the best things in life, Shawn, not me."

"You're such an idealist," Shawn sneered. "And I don't need your Jesus."

"Everyone needs Jesus," Gabe replied softly. He knew internally that arguing with Shawn wouldn't get him anywhere and probably wouldn't change the outcome tonight. Gabe was going to die in a few short hours— maybe even within minutes. He could see that reality reflected in Shawn's eyes. It was only a matter of time. But Gabe hoped that if he planted a few seeds for his old friend to think about through his words and actions then maybe, just maybe, at some point, Shawn would remember this night and surrender his life to Jesus. If that actually occurred, his death would not be in vain.

Shawn sat down and crossed his legs, totally at ease. Apparently, he still had more to say, so Gabe decided that asking a few questions wouldn't go amiss. "So, you're the one that sent the shooter to our office?"

Shawn nodded. "That's right. I used the name of a dead friend and hired a poor excuse for a bomb-maker and then had to send in someone who was, despite his claims, apparently not very skilled, to clean up the mess. Don't worry. I've made better choices since then, but you've still proven exceedingly hard to kill."

"Why kill me at all?"

Cameron shrugged. "Quite frankly, you knew too much about my organization, even if you didn't realize it. I knew it was only a matter of time before the FBI or some other law enforcement agency started dragging details out of you that would only hurt me, so you had to go, as well as the real estate agency itself. I knew the servers would self-destruct due to the encryption I had installed, but the bomb was my backup plan, just in case."

"But all those innocent people got hurt! And if the bomb had gone off, you would have killed or maimed countless others, not only on the third floor, but throughout the building."

Shawn waved his hand. "Collateral damage has never interested me. However, it was a shame to lose Southern Properties. That business was such a great way to launder money. It will take me some time to establish a similar funnel in another venue."

"Laundering money from what?" Gabe asked. He figured as long as he was going to die, he might as well know why.

Shawn smiled an evil smile. "I have my fingers in several pots." He glanced around at his bodyguards, obviously not feeling comfortable divulging too much in front of them. "Suffice it to say, governments and rebel factions both have been very pleased to do business with me, across Europe and even in Africa." He uncrossed his legs and leaned forward. "For the sake of our friendship, I've decided to grant you one last request. What would you like before you die? A good steak dinner? A chance to say goodbye to your FBI agent friend? Name it, and it's yours."

A ball of stress spiked in Gabe's stomach, making nausea rise in his throat. Knowing death was coming was a bitter pill to swallow, and he couldn't deny it. He was scared. There was so much more he had wanted to accomplish in his life. Why had he spent so many hours working instead of developing his friendships and valuing the people around him when he'd had the chance? Why hadn't he reconciled with Tessa earlier?

Why hadn't he drawn closer to Jesus?

Regret pierced him as images from his life flitted across his mind's eye. He had made so many mistakes, and now he would never have time to rectify them.

His thoughts turned to Shawn, who was watching him closely. What should he ask for as a last request? At this point, there was only one thing he really desired. "I want to talk to Agent McIntyre at the FBI." He'd told her he loved her only once since they had been together in Atlanta. He wondered if he said the words again, if she would respond in kind. But whether she did or not, it really didn't matter. He just wanted to hear her voice one more time before he died, regardless of how she replied. He wanted to tell her one last time that he loved her, even if she didn't answer him at all. He needed her to know that there had never been anyone else in his life that had filled that giant hole when he had left Chicago. That she was the light in his life that brought him more happiness than he ever deserved.

The ceiling suddenly exploded with a loud thundering boom. The noise startled Gabe so badly that he jumped and almost knocked over the chair that he was strapped against. Pieces of ceiling tiles, dust and debris fell all around them, but that wasn't all that came from above. Six FBI agents, all dressed in battle gear, including helmets and bullet-proof vests, had entered from above and descended rapidly down long ropes with their guns drawn. Shawn and his bodyguards were so surprised that the FBI was able to disarm them all quickly and efficiently without firing the first shot.

After all were handcuffed, another group of FBI agents entered. They had been in other parts of the building monitoring the mission. Tessa McIntyre led the pack in as agents led the bodyguards out. She stopped in front of Shawn Parker, AKA Bryce Cameron, who was handcuffed and now had two FBI agents on either side of him, holding his arms.

"Shawn Parker, or should I say Bryce Cameron? It's so good to finally meet you face-to-face. There's something I've been wanting to say to you for a very long time."

Shawn gave her a smile that was mostly the bravado of a man who was trying his best to look tough in a difficult situation. "Oh, really? And what might that be?"

She met his eye. "You're under arrest." She nodded to the agents that flanked him. "Read him his rights and get him out of here," she ordered. They complied as she turned toward Gabe and pulled a knife from her belt. She deftly cut the ties that were holding him to the chair, first his hands, then his feet. He stretched, easing the soreness out of his joints that had been forced to stay in one position for far too long.

"Are you okay?" she asked, her tone filled with concern as she helped him to his feet.

"I am now," he said softly. "Thank you for coming to my rescue."

She gave him a tender smile, that even lit

her eyes. "You're welcome. I love you. I had to make sure you knew that."

"I do," Gabe confirmed. "And I love you right back."

EPILOGUE

"That was fantastic!" Tessa declared as they closed and locked the doors of Gabe's small, sporty sedan. They had stopped at one of the large Atlanta churches that was presenting a living nativity scene for Christmas and had enjoyed hearing the Christmas story read and acted out live in front of them as they moved from section to section through the amazing display. The presentation had started with Herod's order for the census, then moved through several other acts that had culminated in a small barn with a manger in the front, clearly visible to all the onlookers. Live donkeys, lambs and even a small camel stood around the actors as they proclaimed the birth of Jesus. In the mother's arms, they had a small baby playing the role of the Christ child who gurgled and cooed at the audience. The scene was breathtaking and heartwarming all at the same time.

After they were at the live nativity presentation, Gabe and Tessa had driven over and parked at the Atlanta Botanical Garden and were about to enter through the premium ticket admission entrance in the visitor's center.

"I totally agree." Gabe smiled. "There's nothing like a living nativity scene to bring home the truth about what Christmas is all about." He put his arm around her waist and walked with her through the gate. "Ready for some Christmas lights?"

A one-way path had been created that winded around the garden, and the seasonal show *Garden Nights, Holiday Lights* began immediately as they entered the three-hundred-acre park. Millions of lights shone along the pathway, and Tessa couldn't wait to see them. "Some people at the office told me about this attraction, but it's even better than I imagined," she gushed as Gabe pocketed the ticket stubs that the attendant had handed him back when they'd gone through the entrance. "They've lit up all of the pathways throughout the garden, and there's supposed to be a giant twenty-seven-foot tree in the middle that is also lit up."

Gabe laughed and touched her nose playfully. "You sound like this is your first Christmas."

"It's the first of many that I get to share with you, now that we've found each other again. I want it to be special."

"As do I." They walked down the path and through the Tunnel of Light, then under canopies of hardwood trees, all well-lit with twinkling lights. Teal and blue miniature bulbs illuminated a stretch of crepe myrtles, and once Gabe and Tessa made it to the tall tree next to the fountain in the middle of the park, they just stood in wonder of the enchanting, illuminated patterns that flitted across the branches. Festive Christmas music played lightly in the background, and as they continued, they came across the Nature's Wonder display where the lights were actually synchronized to the music.

Tessa couldn't remember ever being happier. Of all of the places all over the world, she was right where she desired most to be—in Gabriel Grayson's arms.

As peaceful as the scene was that was playing out in front of them, Gabe had trouble putting the upheaval of the past few days behind him. He imagined it would be months before the trauma subsided, but at least he had a beautiful woman, on the inside and the outside, by his side and ready to help. He was still trying to come to terms with the fact that Shawn, a person who he'd thought was a friend, had used him so egregiously. However, just like Tessa, he was slowly learning that he needed to forgive and move on rather than wallowing in anger or the pain that Shawn's betrayal had caused.

It was hard not to become cynical after everything he had gone through. He'd seen his best friend mastermind audacious financial schemes to cover up his illegal activities with absolutely no regard for human life. As the true breadth of Shawn's holdings were uncovered, as well as the vast network of companies and schemes he was involved in, the FBI had discovered a myriad of illegal activities that reached into areas they had never investigated, including global banks that seemed to condone international fraud and deception on a massive scale. Was there no end to the wickedness? Yet, his God was a big God, and the FBI was working feverishly in conjunction with several international organizations to stop the illegal activities and had already made amazing progress. There was a great deal of optimism that the rule of law would prevail and the guilty would be punished for their crimes. It was Gabe's most fervent desire that as the FBI and their partners proceeded, Shawn's huge criminal enterprise would come crashing to a halt, once and for all. Although there were probably several criminals that wished to step into Cameron's shoes, Gabe was hopeful that the entire enterprise would be crushed by the time the FBI finished their investigation.

He squeezed Tessa's hand and let her warmth flow into him. One good thing had come from all of this. The two had decided to put the past behind them and start fresh with their relationship. Tonight was their first date, and although Tessa would have little spare time in the weeks to come due to her impending promotion and her work on the Cameron case, she had vowed to make as much time as possible to spend with him.

In his professional life, Gabe had already had a job offer from one of his former competitors, but was putting off any career decisions until after the new year. He knew he couldn't stay in real estate, though. Due to Bryce and the Southern Properties case, his old identity as Gabriel Grayson had been compromised. Thankfully, the marshals were working with him to create a new identity in the city of their choice that would allow him to continue his relationship with Tessa.

For now, he just wanted to pause, take a moment and enjoy being with Tessa. There would be time later for the two of them to figure out their future and decide on the details. As long as they were together, he was confident the rest would fall into place. He stopped along the path and she gave him a questioning look, but he just smiled, then pulled her close. His lips met hers in a gentle kiss, and he shivered involuntarily at the knowledge that the flame of love was still alive between them.

"Thank you," he said softly as he caressed her cheek. "You saved my life but also reminded me what's important in life."

"You did the same for me," she replied, a smile in her eyes that reflected the shimmering lights around them. "My career is a big part of my life, just like yours, but people are what matter. We're supposed to love God and love others, and I needed that reminder. I'm so glad you're back in my life. I missed you so much."

Gabe kissed her again, his heart light with possibilities. "God willing, we'll have several years to explore all the ways we can show love to each other and to the ones around us."

"I can't wait!" Tessa agreed. "If God is for us, who can be against us?"

* * * * *

Dear Reader,

As we've lived through the pandemic, we've been reminded that God never promises any of us an easy life. In fact, in John 16:33, it's clear that we will face tribulation. Even missionaries and those who have dedicated their lives to serving God still go through difficult situations. Remember Paul from the New Testament? He was shipwrecked and imprisoned, and even snakebitten! Yet despite these trials, he still continued his work for the Lord and even shared Jesus with the prison guards. Joseph in the Old Testament was also imprisoned and was able to save an entire nation! What Gabe and Tessa both learned in this book is that God is in control, despite their difficult circumstances.

So, when you go through difficult times, take a look at James 1:2, and consider it all joy when you encounter various trials. It may not be easy to get through the situation, but God promises you will never go through difficulties alone. Philippians 4:6-7 says, "Do not be anxious about anything, but in everything by prayer and supplication with thanksgiving let your requests be made known to

God. And the peace of God, which surpasses all understanding, will guard your hearts and your minds in Christ Jesus."

Please visit my website www.Kathleen-Tailer.com to see my other books and to take advantage of the Bible studies available to help you draw closer to Jesus. I love to hear from my readers! Please also check out my Facebook page (https://www.facebook.com/ktailer/) and leave me a note.

May God bless you!
Kathleen Tailer

Get 4 FREE REWARDS!

We'll send you 2 FREE Books plus 2 FREE Mystery Gifts.

Love Inspired Suspense books showcase how courage and optimism unite in stories of faith and love in the face of danger.

FREE Value Over $20

YES! Please send me 2 FREE Love Inspired Suspense novels and my 2 FREE mystery gifts (gifts are worth about $10 retail). After receiving them, if I don't wish to receive any more books, I can return the shipping statement marked "cancel." If I don't cancel, I will receive 6 brand-new novels every month and be billed just $5.24 each for the regular-print edition or $5.99 each for the larger-print edition in the U.S., or $5.74 each for the regular-print edition or $6.24 each for the larger-print edition in Canada. That's a savings of at least 13% off the cover price. It's quite a bargain! Shipping and handling is just 50¢ per book in the U.S. and $1.25 per book in Canada.* I understand that accepting the 2 free books and gifts places me under no obligation to buy anything. I can always return a shipment and cancel at any time. The free books and gifts are mine to keep no matter what I decide.

Choose one: ☐ **Love Inspired Suspense Regular-Print** (153/353 IDN GNWN) ☐ **Love Inspired Suspense Larger-Print** (107/307 IDN GNWN)

Name (please print)

Address   Apt. #

City   State/Province   Zip/Postal Code

Email: Please check this box ☐ if you would like to receive newsletters and promotional emails from Harlequin Enterprises ULC and its affiliates. You can unsubscribe anytime.

Mail to the **Harlequin Reader Service:**
IN U.S.A.: P.O. Box 1341, Buffalo, NY 14240-8531
IN CANADA: P.O. Box 603, Fort Erie, Ontario L2A 5X3

Want to try 2 free books from another series? Call 1-800-873-8635 or visit www.ReaderService.com.

---

*Terms and prices subject to change without notice. Prices do not include sales taxes, which will be charged (if applicable) based on your state or country of residence. Canadian residents will be charged applicable taxes. Offer not valid in Quebec. This offer is limited to one order per household. Books received may not be as shown. Not valid for current subscribers to Love Inspired Suspense books. All orders subject to approval. Credit or debit balances in a customer's account(s) may be offset by any other outstanding balance owed by or to the customer. Please allow 4 to 6 weeks for delivery. Offer available while quantities last.

Your Privacy—Your information is being collected by Harlequin Enterprises ULC, operating as Harlequin Reader Service. For a complete summary of the information we collect, how we use this information and to whom it is disclosed, please visit our privacy notice located at corporate.harlequin.com/privacy-notice. From time to time we may also exchange your personal information with reputable third parties. If you wish to opt out of this sharing of your personal information, please visit readerservice.com/consumerchoice or call 1-800-873-8635. **Notice to California Residents**—Under California law, you have specific rights to control and access your data. For more information on these rights and how to exercise them, visit corporate.harlequin.com/california-privacy.

LIS21R2

Get 4 FREE REWARDS!

We'll send you 2 FREE Books plus 2 FREE Mystery Gifts.

Harlequin Heartwarming Larger-Print books will connect you to uplifting stories where the bonds of friendship, family and community unite.

FREE
Value Over
$20

HARLEQUIN SELECTS COLLECTION

19 FREE BOOKS IN ALL!

From Robyn Carr to RaeAnne Thayne to Linda Lael Miller and Sherryl Woods we promise (actually, GUARANTEE!) each author in the Harlequin Selects collection has seen their name on the *New York Times* or *USA TODAY* bestseller lists!